I really don't remember too much what it was like, walking that long span under the drizzly sky that day, the river churning so far below me, the wind light but gusty. I mostly remember I was scared to death, absolutely terrified. I could hardly breathe, but kept my legs moving, one in front of the other. I tried not to look down, toward the river, tried to keep in mind that it was Elijah's dark head below me on the bridge side, that I was safe.

But I wasn't perfectly safe, and I knew it.

Rimwalkers

VICKI GROVE

The Putnam & Grosset Group

ACKNOWLEDGMENTS

Farming is a very technically complicated profession. I'd like to thank the following expert farmers, who graciously read this manuscript and offered technical advice:

Dave, Jo, and Sandi Beeman; my dad, James Baum; Paul Singer and the other "country people" in the Sedalia Writers' Group; and the employees of the Sedalia, Missouri, Farmers Home Administration, especially Beverly Dillon.

I'd also like to thank Mrs. Carder's sixth grade at Cameron, Missouri, who adopted me the year this book was being written.

And it's high time I thanked my wonderful editor, Anne O'Connell.

Library of Congress Cataloging-in-Publication Data
Grove, Vicki. Rimwalkers/Vicki Grove.   p.   cm.   Summary: As she
develops a closeness with two cousins during a summer on her grandparents' farm in Illinois, fourteen-year-old Victoria emerges from the
shadow of her showy younger sister and has some experiences that
change her life forever. [1. Sisters—Fiction. 2. Cousins—Fiction. 3.
Self-perception—Fiction. 4. Farm life—Fiction.] I. Title. II. Title:
Rimwalkers. PZ7.G9275Ri   1993   [Fic]—dc20   92-36091   CIP
AC ISBN 0-698-11423-X
1   3   5   7   9   10   8   6   4   2

For my parents—
who are always trying to give me things,
though they really gave me everything
a long time ago.

The Farm

"*Do you believe in magic?*"

It's been almost twenty years, but still I can hear Rennie's quick, breathless voice, asking the question.

And just as clearly, I hear myself, fourteen and sure of things, laughing at him, politely. I was already a scientist that summer in every important way but one. I only believed in rocks and fossils, in insects and bird feathers and snake-skins, in things of the earth that I could hold in my hands.

Yes, I remember Rennie's voice, and almost as well I remember the light that summer at the farm. It was so strangely golden-yellow, full of floating pollen and dust motes. It seemed thick enough to carry things, thick enough to blast like a solid cylinder through the hinged door of the hayloft I used as my field lab. It glazed the round windows in the attic of our great-great-grandparents' ruined house down the road until Elijah and Rennie and I were dizzy from trying to peer through it. It spun itself lazily through the doors of the tentlike playhouse Sara made from quilts in the branches of the apricot trees. The light didn't just exist around us so much as it seemed to cover us, to cling to us so we almost glowed with it, almost felt sticky with it.

It's tempting to blame what happened that summer partly on that light. Maybe it made us feel invulnerable, or even immortal.

Or maybe I should be ashamed, shifting the blame even partly to the light.

Nearly twenty years have passed, and now I am a scientist, a geologist. And still when I remember that summer, there are so many questions, so many questions.

And in my dreams I sometimes hear Rennie's voice that bright but moonless first night of July.

"Do you believe in magic?"

I could have told him no, and been sure of that for the last time in my life.

But I didn't think Rennie could really be serious, and I can't remember ever answering him at all.

Chapter 1

Sara didn't want to spend that summer at our grandparents' farm in the first place. She kept thinking she could talk our parents out of the idea. But as the last week of school arrived and then began to reel by without Daddy giving an inch, I could see panic building in her eyes.

On Wednesday night Daddy came home from work with their airline tickets to Ireland and our bus tickets to Illinois, and Sara was forced to realize the matter was settled. Still, she woke up Thursday morning grouchy.

"Heritage, shmeritage," she muttered, then groaned at herself in our full-length mirror and stomped on into the bathroom.

Without even stopping to put on my glasses, I slid from my bed and bounded across the room to grab my chance at the mirror while she was gone. Since I was several inches taller than she was and since the top of our mirror was lined with photographs of her friends,

I crouched to see myself—my sharp, freckled cheek-bones, my tan hair, my long thin neck and pointed elbows. I squeezed my hair back into a rubber band.

"How can you be smiling like that?" Sara clomped back in wearing a towel, her thick dark hair dripping.

"What?" I squinted at my reflection. Sure enough—I was smiling.

Sara's reflection joined mine, only hers was glaring. "You wouldn't be smiling if you were the one who had to leave behind your friends and your life for the entire summer."

I could have pointed out that I was, after all, going to the farm for the summer too. But since we both knew what she meant, I decided to answer her original question instead.

"I suppose I'm smiling because the only nerve-wracking thing I have left this week is the honors assembly this afternoon," I answered, figuring it out as I went. "But mostly, I guess I can hardly believe we're leaving in only four more days. Four days, and then I'll have three perfect months working on my collections from my field lab at the farm."

"Four tiny days, then three gruesome months!" Sara moaned, nudging me aside with her hip and reaching for her hair dryer. "It sounds like an eternity. I'll lose three whole months of practice on cheers and diving and stuff!"

She bent at the waist, flipped her head down with a snap that splattered the mirror with drips, and buried her dryer inside the long dangle of her upside-down hair.

"Mom and Daddy deserve this trip to Ireland alone, Sara," I said, figuring she probably couldn't hear me. It didn't matter—she knew all this as well as I did. "They've saved forever, and they never even had a honeymoon."

"I know, I know," she called over the whine of the dryer. "I just don't see why I can't stay here in Milwaukee with Rachelle or Diane, instead of wasting away in boring old Illinois."

We'd never spent more than a few days at the farm at one time, and Daddy really wanted us to get to know our heritage. But I didn't dare use that word "heritage" again. After all, she'd woken up groaning from Daddy using it at supper last night.

"Listen," I suggested instead, picking up my glasses and tucking the arms under the tightly stretched sides of my hair, "maybe you should consider the things you could look forward to at the farm."

"Name one," she growled, then straightened quickly and whirled to point accusingly toward me with the dryer. "And, Victoria—studying bugs and that other yucky stuff you like doesn't count!"

"Okay, then how about this. You could set up a music studio for yourself. Mr. McEwen is always saying how much natural ability you have. Musicians go on retreats sometimes, seal themselves away in some place of nature to feed their spirits. You could use the summer to become a virtuoso trombone player."

She turned back toward the mirror, still frowning, and began slowly rolling her bangs around the bristles of her brush. "How good could I get in three months? What's virtuoso? Good enough to be the first seventh-grader ever to march with the eighth-grade band when I start junior high next fall?"

I shrugged. "Without your friends constantly calling you and interrupting your concentration, I'd say anything is possible."

When I left soon after that to catch my bus to Symington Junior High, she was still at the mirror, but no longer frowning quite so much. Now she was looking dreamily into her own eyes, obviously picturing herself in the gold and purple uniform of the Symington Marching Eagles.

The honors assembly that afternoon was as nerve-wracking as I'd expected. First they gave the athletic awards, then the music awards, then the club awards. It was nearly 2:00 by the time they got to the academic awards, and most of the kids were slouched far down in their metal seats. A couple of seventh-grade boys had fallen completely out, onto the hard gym floor. They snorted with pleasure when everybody turned to laugh at them.

By the time Mr. Hartley walked to the stage, my ears were ringing and I could hardly breathe. I found myself imagining the well-intentioned but embarrassing speech he was about to give.

"And now, I'd like to present to you Miss Tory Ann Moore," he intoned in my mind. "Outstanding scientist, future Ph.D., and all-around quiet but exemplary student whom you should all get to know a little better and . . ."

My excruciating thoughts were interrupted as Mr. Hartley cleared his throat and began to speak. "This year's eighth-grade science award goes to Victoria Moore," he said, simply. A few people applauded in the bored, thumping way they'd applauded the last few things.

I took a deep breath, and tried to pretend I was invisible inside a safe cocoon as I made it up the aisle, up the wooden stairs, took my medal, said "Thank you" to Mr. Hartley, and, watching my feet, went quickly back to my aisle, to my row, to my seat.

My hands were shaking, and when I looked at my medal it seemed almost embedded in my palm and I saw my fingers had little white dots all over them.

When I got off the bus that afternoon, our front yard was filled with Sara and her friends. They were bouncing around more or less in formation, kicking and clapping, yelling.

"Hey, Victoria! There you are! Hi! Hi! Hi! Guess what?"

Sara ran to me and grabbed my hand, jumping up and down, her eyes like small pieces of the bright spring sky. Her grumpiness from the morning was as gone as an evaporated cloud.

"They announced who made cheerleaders, and you guys were on the list," I said, stating the obvious.

"All of us! We ARE the Symington Junior High seventh-grade cheerleading team for next year! Us and a couple of other girls."

My mother was on the porch, leaning against the screen door, watching the cheerleading and smiling happily. When she saw me looking at her she jerked upright as though caught in the act of something. She smiled even more broadly, so broadly her face no longer looked happy but now looked painfully stretched. She pantomimed holding something between the fingers of her right hand and jiggling it, so I dug in my sweater pocket, walked up the sidewalk that bisected our yard, and handed my medal to her.

"Oh, honey, we're so, so proud of you! This is just the greatest, Victoria! Just simply wonderful!" She held the medal in her left hand and hugged me with her right arm, but after a second or two I felt my neck burning and shrugged away.

"It's really not that big a deal. I've known I was getting it for a week, and there were a zillion awards given at the assembly."

She followed me inside the house, going on and on. "Well, it most certainly IS a big deal. Your dad is going to want to take pictures of you holding that medal so don't you put it away. It's not just every day that . . ."

I stopped walking and turned to her in the dark hallway. "It's not just every day that I'm the one to get an award? Mom, it's okay. Go back outside and watch the cheering. It doesn't bother me when you

14

. . . I mean, when people, when anybody, appreciates Sara. I'm used to being Sara Moore's big sister."

I went on down the hall, but when I reached the door to our room I could sense that she was still standing motionless behind me, so I turned back to her and smiled.

"Really! And don't be afraid to congratulate her around me, okay? Sara always deserves the gushing when people gush."

In our room I changed into my lab uniform of old jeans and a paint-stained t-shirt. Then, when I heard her footsteps and knew Mom had finally left the hallway, I slipped out to the little science lab I had behind the paint storage shelves in the garage.

I spent most of the rest of the evening loading my microscope and insects into the special wooden collecting box Daddy had made me for the trip. I intended to take only a quick break for dinner, but I lost some time because afterwards Daddy insisted I pose for a bunch of pictures with the medal.

On Friday, everything at school just sort of collapsed in a nerve-wracking jumble of paper airplanes and water balloons. I came home exhausted, but Sara seemed supercharged, though teary-eyed from saying good-bye to her friends.

When she walked in the front door, she was carrying two trombone cases.

"Mine!" she said, clunking the one in her left hand down on the floor. "And the one Mr. McEwen is lending me for the summer!" She clunked down the one in her right hand.

Mom and I stared at the cases for a few seconds, then Mom asked the obvious question. "Two?"

Sara brightened up, shrugged out of her backpack, and began doing the movements to cheers there in the hallway while she talked. "I told Mr. McEwen my plan to devote myself to my music at the farm this summer, to become a vortismo? And he got, like, all impressed and excited and told me I should also be practicing on a horn with an F trigger, so he lent me one! Give me an F! Give me an F! Give me an F, F, F! Trigger! Trigger! Yea!"

She jumped into the air, kicking both cases lightly as she left the ground, and both slipped quietly and without resistance over onto their sides like small, mortally wounded animals.

"A vortismo?" Mom asked me.

"I think she means virtuoso," I said.

Chapter 2

We packed all day Saturday, and Sara said her last long telephone good-byes to her friends. Early the next morning, our parents took us to the Greyhound station, and tearfully saw us off before leaving for the airport themselves.

The bus trip from Milwaukee to Mulberry Grove, Illinois, seemed long, and hot. Sitting beside Sara and her trombone cases for three hundred and sixty miles was like sharing a two-person seat with three other people. Still, I suffered in silence till we were almost there, when seven hours on the bus had made us both too grouchy for good manners to hold any longer. Then I shoved hard and meaningfully at her trombones with my knee.

"Watch it!" she said, then—"Yuck, I can smell your bugs."

"You couldn't possibly," I informed her. "What you smell is diesel fuel from the bus." I squirmed closer toward the window to get more comfortable.

"Why couldn't you have let the man stick those things under the bus with the rest of our luggage instead of keeping them inside here with us?"

She looked at me like I'd suddenly gone crazy, her blue eyes round with horror beneath her thick, dark lashes. She wrapped one arm around each of her trombone cases and pulled them closer to her, like they were two of the tangly-haired, frowsy dolls she still played with when nobody but me was around to see.

"You brought your smelly bug stuff inside with us," she said.

"That's different." I tapped my heels, and beneath my feet my wooden collecting box felt solid and secure. "Under the bus it's hot, and some wings might fall off or something."

"Under the bus, my slide oil might evaporate," she said.

I smiled at that, in spite of myself. I knew Sara knew nothing whatsoever about slide oil, but it was always hard not to admire her sassy, never-give-an-inch attitude.

She smiled back and bounced in her seat. "I can't wait to set up my studio! I'm going to practice for just hours and hours every day! I'll just get so incredibly, incredibly good, good, good! Give me a G, give me a G, give me an O-O-D!"

She didn't have room to do even the arm actions to a cheer, so she reached back and began braiding her hair instead.

18

I looked out my window, but the glare of the sun made it hard to see the countryside. About all I could see was a dazzle of light from the thick lenses of my glasses, so I turned to look past Sara, out the glareless window across the aisle. The rolling hills of Wisconsin had given way to much flatter ground, ground divided into huge squares of gold and green. Tractors looking like determined ants patiently pulled huge plows across those nearly endless fields, under a huge sky with dabs of white cloud.

"Okay, now tell me again which one of our two cousins is going to be at the farm with us," Sara suddenly demanded. "Oren or Elijah?"

I sighed, put my head back against the top of my seat, and closed my eyes. She knew it was Elijah as well as I did, but she wanted a chance to talk about Oren. "Elijah. Since he's grown up on a farm, he's going to be helping Grandpa out this summer."

"I wish it was Oren," Sara murmured. Surprise, surprise. Oren's daredevil life just fascinated her. Aunt Crystal had been calling from San Diego a lot lately to cry on Daddy's shoulder about Oren, and Sara always hurried into the hall and eavesdropped on every word of their conversations.

"Oren must be super cool," she continued, "and I can't even remember this boring old Elijah."

It was hard for me to believe Sara didn't remember Elijah, though she'd been claiming she didn't ever since Daddy had told us Elijah was going to be at the farm with us. Elijah and Aunt Lydia and Uncle John

19

had spent a week at our house five years before on their way somewhere from their farm in Missouri. As I remembered, Sara had pestered Elijah the whole time to swing her, to ride her on the back of a bike, or just to pay attention to her.

"You'll remember Elijah when you see him. You've never even MET Oren. Neither of us have. And Elijah's not boring, just quiet."

"I thought you told me he was just like you," Sara said.

She never meant to be insulting with comments like that, so I let it pass. I looked back out the window and laughed a sarcastic laugh. "Oren has even dropped out of school, and he's only sixteen. I'm so sure it would be just WONDERFUL having somebody like that hulking around all the time this summer."

She didn't say anything back, so I turned to her.

"Really, Sara, Elijah's nice. Don't worry about meeting him."

"You're the one who worries about meeting people, not me," she mumbled, which was so true I didn't bother to respond.

Instead, I spent the last half hour of the trip thinking about that week five years before when I'd gotten to know my cousin Elijah. In fact, a part of me had been remembering that week ever since Daddy had told us Elijah would be at the farm.

Elijah and I were both nine years old the week of that visit, and we didn't talk much to each other or to anybody else. But when we could escape Sara and the laughing, chattering grown-ups, we sought each other's company. It seemed so natural a thing to do that we didn't question it. He came onto the porch once while I was sitting on the steps, and without exchanging a word we both just got up and walked down to the little creek near our house to look for tadpoles. I walked up to him once when he was pushing Sara in the swing. With fingers crossed behind my back, I told Sara Mom was calling her, and Elijah and I waited for her to get inside the house before we collapsed in giggles together as though we'd planned that trick for days.

Three or four times, again without discussing it, Elijah and I walked to the corner Dairy Freeze and got one banana popsicle, which we split. Lots of times I would be sitting on the sidewalk in front of our house playing jacks and he'd come up and sit beside me with a hammer and a roll of caps, and we'd explode them together. Or he'd be tightening the chain on one of the bikes and I'd sit on the curb and simply watch.

For weeks, maybe months, after Elijah went home, I woke in the night sometimes, remembering the way he would put a banana popsicle on the sidewalk, break it cleanly with a karate chop, then pull the two sticks from the wrapper and hand one frosted, sun-colored half to me. It was always so cold it hurt my teeth, but it tasted so good it was more like eating a feeling of happiness than just a kind of food.

One of the trombones drooped over onto my side of the seat. Halfheartedly this time, I shoved at it with my knee.

"Sara, uh, listen." I cleared my throat. "Do you think while we're here at the farm you could just . . . call me Tory?"

Sara wrinkled her nose and laughed. "No way! You're a natural-born Victoria."

"Why do you say that?" I asked her, peeved. No one was "born" an anything.

"For one thing, a Tory would just be a Tory and wouldn't have to ask people to call her that." Her trombones sagged toward me again. "Besides, you'll never get up the nerve to actually tell people your name is Tory, so why worry about it?"

The speaker crackled on and the bus driver spoke. "Next stop, Mulberry Grove. Passengers getting off at Mulberry Grove should begin to collect their belongings."

"Better get your yucky bugs," Sara said matter-of-factly, hugging her trombones.

Chapter 3

Wade Huffmeyer, our grandfather's hired man, picked us up at Mulberry Grove for the twelve-mile ride to the farm. Gram had already explained over the phone that the last week of May was such a busy planting week that whoever could get away from the fields easiest would be there to meet us.

Sara and I usually spent at least a couple of week-ends a year at the farm with our parents, so we knew Wade pretty well and really liked him. He was skinny and funny, and reminded both of us of the Scarecrow in the movie *The Wizard of Oz.*

"How's Luther doing?" Sara asked when we were loaded into Wade's old green pickup and on our way out of Mulberry Grove.

At the sound of his name, Wade's big, slobbering hound dog suddenly reared up from the little storage space behind the seat, where he'd evidently been sleeping. Wade reached back, laughing, and scratched him, and Luther hung his head happily over Sara's part of our seat and began snuffling her ear.

"Looky there, Sara, he remembers you from clear before!" Wade's dark reddish eyes crinkled at the corners.

"Everybody always remembers Sara," I told him, then I sighed contentedly and settled back to look out the window. I loved the green and dusty drive along this road. I loved to gradually slip into the sights and smells of the farm, like I was slipping into a new skin, a skin I really liked much better than the one I had to wear in the city. Something about this area felt old to me, old as bones. Old as my own bones, and settled as deeply inside me.

"Sometimes when it seems kind of quietlike to us in our cabin in the woods at night, Luther and me, we turn on the television set," Wade was saying. "I like those detective shows, but Luther—well, he prefers commercials. You know, the ones where the animals dress up in clothes or dance around with their owners or even sing or talk?"

"Those commercials for pet food," Sara said.

"Yes, those are the ones. Well, I'll be darned, Sara, if I haven't caught Luther sneaking off by himself to practice his dancing lately. There he'll be, that big old skinny thing, tiptoeing around the kitchen on two feet like he thinks he's a Hollywood star!"

I rolled my eyes and smiled slightly to be polite, but kept my attention out the window, where fields and streams were sliding past, and deep green fencerows of elm and oak and hackberry trees fringed the sky. The landscape was dotted with white wood or red brick farmhouses, all with gleaming aluminum buildings behind them—round grain storage silos, rectangular barns and sheds. Occasionally a very old barn would stand alone, stained red or left with its bare oak wood to weather. Probably there had been houses by those barns once, old houses torn down. Houses were probably less necessary than barns out here in many ways, less lasting.

"Now, Luther, what do you have to say for your silly old self?" Sara asked, giggling. I turned to see her holding him by the ears while he slobbered and trembled and gazed adoringly into her eyes. No matter how silly dogs sometimes looked, they seemed totally unself-conscious.

A thought drifted through my head as the fields were drifting by Wade's pickup—if I could live here all the time I probably wouldn't often feel self-conscious, either.

I shifted to lean forward a little in my seat. We were coming to the part of the country known as Irishtown, though it wasn't a town. It was a green, forested area of a few square miles where lots of people from Ireland had settled in this part of Illinois in the nineteenth century, including Sara's and my ancestors, the McNeills.

And it was there—right there at the border of Irishtown when Wade turned off the asphalt road that Gram called the "hard road" and turned onto the

25

gravel road that would take us the next four miles through forest and fields to the farm—it was there that the light changed and began to come down on us like sifted gold.

"Almost home," I whispered, and was immediately embarrassed. My home was in Milwaukee, not out here.

But the others didn't hear. Or for that matter, didn't seem to notice the strange change in the light, either.

"I just know I can train Luther to do a dog somersault." Sara was chattering, chattering. Her voice faded out to a background hum then reappeared when I paid a little attention, like a radio turned down, then back up. "Danielle has her two cats doing jumps with her when she cheers, almost at the exactly right times, too."

Luther sneezed and shook his ears hard. We all laughed and our eyes filled with tears, partly from the road dust filling the truck as the gravel crunched beneath Wade's tires.

We passed McKendree Chapel Cemetery, and turned onto Chapel Hill Ridge. I put my hands on the dashboard and strained forward, eager for my first glimpse of the farm tucked into the valley below that high ledge of road.

And then there it was, below us and a mile in the distance, the big pillared house set like a white diamond amidst acres and acres of golden wheat and deep green woods and meadows. Ivy-covered oak barns and silos trailed along beside it on three sides, and the apricot orchard was in full bloom beyond the side yard—a pink cloud. The other white house, the homestead house of my great-great-grandparents', was just visible on this side of the orchard, closely surrounded by huge trees and overgrown bramble bushes. One of the two round attic windows seemed to wink at me like an eye in the thick, golden sunlight.

A feeling of total happiness settled into me, seemed to fill me from the lungs on out as I breathed that golden air.

"Home," I thought again, and this time forgot to correct myself.

Gram and Grandpa's six-pillared house was built on a little hill and set far off the road, so when you turned into the long, banked driveway you saw the house looming not only ahead of you but also slightly over you, spreading the winglike sides of its wrap-around porch like an elegant white bird. Orchards and gardens were set close to the house on all sides, and there was a big circular driveway right by the kitchen door with a goldfish pond in the middle. The pond was surrounded by willow trees and smooth, flat stones—"sitting stones" Gram called them, because everyone seemed drawn to sit on them, to watch the fish or to just lazily gaze at their own reflections.

Wade stopped the truck by the goldfish pond and got out to take our luggage from the back. Sara leaned impatiently across me to open our door, and scrambled over me and out before I could move. I watched her go toward our grandmother, who had just burst from the kitchen door and was hurrying to meet us, waving both hands and laughing out loud.

Sara ran into her short, plump arms, and both of them reeled off the narrow sidewalk and nearly fell, hugging, laughing.

"Land's sake, Sara Jean, you've gotten even prettier since we were up to see you Christmas!" Gram was shouting as I approached them. "And, Victoria Ann, my, but except for that sandy hair you look more like your father every day!"

She kept one arm tightly around Sara, and reached for me with the other.

"Gram?" I hugged her quickly, then took a step away. "You and Sara go on inside, okay? I just want to walk around once to stretch my legs."

Gram chuckled, and wiped some wisps of flyaway curly hair from her forehead, tucking them neatly to the side under a rhinestone-studded bobby pin. Her blue eyes sparkled like that pin. "Settling in," she said with a wink to my sister. "Victoria's like her father in that, too. Always has to touch all the bases first thing when she comes out here, as if to make sure nothing's changed much about the grounds and farmyard."

Wade was driving off, and I waved him a good-bye. "Your granddad's working in the field still, but he says to say he'll see you come suppertime!" he yelled, and I nodded that I understood.

"Is Elijah with him?" I called back.

But Wade was too far away to hear. And it didn't make any difference, because a few seconds later, as I drifted around the side of the house and toward the apricot orchard, I saw Elijah.

At first I mistook him for one of the college boys from Mulberry Grove that Grandpa hired to load hay bales into wagons in the summer. He was tall—taller by a few inches than me. Twice as tall as he'd been in fourth grade, when his family had visited us for that week. His hair was darker than I remembered—dark as Sara's and our father's. He was standing between two of the squat, wide-branched apricot trees with his back to me, looking across the clover fields and Moccasin Creek, toward our great great-grandparents' old deserted house. He had his hands clasped together behind his head, and his long arms made his elbows seem to puncture the air.

"Hi," I called out, then cleared my throat. "Elijah?"

I suddenly felt my heart racing. What was I doing? He might not even remember me!

Elijah whirled around, surprised. I guess he'd been too lost in his thoughts to hear the truck, or Gram's greeting. I could understand—I was often lost like that too.

That thought someway gave me the courage to walk toward him. I saw that he was very tan, I suspected from field work, so his blue eyes looked even more striking than Sara's did. He shook his head to move the dark hair from them, but not in the careful, cute way Sara sometimes did.

"Victoria, right?" he said quietly, grabbing an apricot blossom and beginning to shred it. He was smiling, but a pinkish stain was moving up both sides of his neck.

"Tory," I said, grabbing my own apricot blossom. "Only Gram still calls me Victoria."

Elijah lowered his eyes to the small pinkish-white flower in his hands. "Gram still calls me Elijah Matthew. Five whole syllables every time she wants me."

I laughed, he glanced at me as though relieved, and we dropped our mangled blossoms and smiled directly at each other.

"Had any banana popsicles lately?" he asked, and I felt like shouting for joy because suddenly it was like it had been five minutes, not five years, since we'd caught those tadpoles and exploded those caps on the sidewalk.

I shook my head and let out a little "nhuh" of laughter; he smiled more broadly, then neither of us said anything. But it was suddenly okay, amazingly okay to just stand there quietly without filling the air with words. Elijah was still Elijah.

"This is sort of weird, huh?" he said after a couple of minutes, sticking his hands in the back pockets of his dusty jeans. "All four of us cousins here at the farm at the same time, for the first time ever?"

"All . . . all four of us? Oren surely isn't here . . . is he?"

"He arrived last night, in the middle of the night." Elijah gestured toward the house behind us with one shoulder, and sure enough—I heard rock music coming from somewhere upstairs.

I felt like I was tumbling, thrown for a loop, disoriented.

"Why? I mean, what's he doing here? I'm sorry, I just mean . . . well, where's Aunt Crystal?"

Elijah shrugged. "He came alone. There were a bunch of phone calls yesterday, then Grandpa picked him up in St. Louis, at the train station. It's all kind of . . . mysterious."

"Had you met him before?"

Elijah shook his head. "I'd never met him till last night. When Aunt Crystal came to Missouri to visit us last Thanksgiving, Oren stayed at home, or somewhere. She said he didn't like to leave the city."

"I've never met him either," I murmured. "Just . . . well, heard about him."

Either Elijah was too polite to ask what I'd heard or, more likely, he'd heard plenty himself. Suddenly, a dull, loud hammering began, and together we ran from the orchard, and hurried to look up at the second floor of the house, where the sound was coming from.

The screen from one of the bedroom windows was bulging out of its casing, and, while we watched, it exploded outward, aluminum frame and all, and went clattering along the porch roof and to the ground, smashing some of Gram's irises. Then out of the empty window casing there appeared two leather boots, followed by two hairy white legs in cut-off jeans, and seconds later a boy with a sleeveless black Grateful Dead t-shirt and curly blond hair was sitting balanced on the edge of the screen-less window, grinning calmly down at us.

"Well, I got our escape route cleared," he called, strumming an invisible guitar while music blared out from behind him. "Now which one of you good little scouts knows how to make a rope ladder so we can break out of this prison at night?"

Chapter 4

Elijah looked slowly from Oren down to the broken screen lying there in the mangled irises. He walked over and picked it up, tucked it under his arm, and headed with long strides toward the barn with it without saying a word.

I was left standing there alone.

I felt like I always did when the kids at school chose ball teams in gym—exposed, totally embarrassed, foolish, and too tall and skinny and awkward. I wanted to run after Elijah, but it would have looked stupid because there was no reason for me to. After all, I was equally related to this Oren, though at the moment he was stranger to me and much, much scarier than any of the so-called "creatures" I'd categorized for my bug collections over the years.

I could feel his eyes on me from above, as if I were the bug and HE was the collector.

"So, Tory, aren't you going to run after Elijah?"

Oren asked, reading my mind for the first, but certainly not the last, time.

"Tory? You called me . . . Tory?"

"It's your name, isn't it? I mean, our grandmother calls you Victoria, but you're really a Tory. Just like I'm a Rennie. Oren—what a laugh."

I was too flustered at the time to be able to really remember now, but maybe I took an automatic step forward, toward the broken clumps of irises.

"You're not going to kneel down there in the grass and try to fix those poor broken flowers, are you?" he asked in a cocky, ridiculing way. I swallowed hard, and took a step backwards, away from the bruised irises. Suddenly, it was important to me that he didn't think I'd do anything uncool, anything a Tory wouldn't do.

"I . . . I just thought . . ." I stammered.

He threw back his head, shook his tight blond curls wildly, and laughed. I felt my neck burning. I kept trying to remember that Oren was a troublemaker, practically a delinquent and flunking out, that I shouldn't feel stupid around him, like I was the idiot and HE was the smart one.

Still, I couldn't talk or look up at him, and a few seconds later he slid down the rough tiles of the roof, let his legs hang over the side, then dropped into the iris bed, landing on his feet and not even taking a hop back for balance.

He was inches from me then, and talked fast. His voice, I noticed, was higher than I'd expected it to be.

"People like you and Eli just kill me, with your ideas of what's right and what's wrong. The 'right' thing to do is the thing that makes you personally strong, period. If I'm going to be trapped in this place then I'm using the summer to work on my main project—myself. Let broken windows and torn-up flowers take care of themselves."

I wanted to angrily ask him why he thought he knew so much about Elijah's ideas, or mine. But instead I just stood there, speechless and grinning. Not grinning because I wanted to, but because my face stretched into that kind of a wide skull-like grin whenever I was totally embarrassed. I'd tried and tried but there was nothing I could do to stop it.

"See you later, little cousin," Oren mumbled, looking at his wrist. He pressed a tiny button on his complicated watch, and took off running down the driveway, to the gravel road.

As I watched him go I noticed I'd had the wrong first impression when I saw him emerge from the window. Probably because his legs were so white, so pale—and because for some reason I found myself looking for similarities between Sara and me and both our cousins—I'd immediately classified him as being "unathletic," like I was. But he was definitely muscular—slightly shorter but much broader-shouldered than tall, wiry Elijah. Also, the way he'd jumped from the roof was catlike in its grace, and now his legs looked hard as pistons as he ran.

When I knew he was too far down the road to see,

I bent to the iris bed and, with shaking hands, tried to straighten the flowers that he had broken.

Everybody was together for the first time at dinner that night, in the little room off the kitchen that Gram jokingly called "the grand dining hall." There were two huge windows in that tiny room, taking up nearly one entire wall. Those windows faced the apricot orchard and the old, ruined house beyond. The sky, by dinnertime, was streaked with the pink clouds of a Midwestern summer sunset, and the fields were filled with shadows.

Grandpa sat at the head of the long, rectangular table, with Wade and Elijah to his right. Sara and Rennie and I sat opposite them, and Gram sat opposite Grandpa, on the side of the table bordering the kitchen. Gram had told us that Wade didn't always eat with us, and when he wasn't there Rennie would take his chair. It was obvious that when Wade was there, though, he needed to be on the less crowded side of the table, to have room for Luther to sit with his chin on his knees, begging food with his droopy, sad eyes.

I was a little worried about having to sit so close to Rennie that first night, having to think of things to say to him after that strange conversation in the yard. But I shouldn't have worried. Sara was obviously totally enchanted by Rennie, and when Sara was enchanted by someone she pulled out all the stops to enchant them right back.

That night she asked Rennie about a million questions, nonstop—most of them designed to give him a glimpse of her own exciting life.

"Did you get your fancy watch for timing yourself while you train? What are you, a swimmer? I'm a swimmer, and I dive. I've got a watch with a stopwatch thing like that on it too, but I left it at home. I brought this watch. See?" She stuck her left arm under Rennie's nose. "All us cheerleaders got them to match. Mine's green, the band I mean. Tammy's is blue, Trisha's is . . ."

"Potatoes, Sara?" Gram said, handing her the bowl meaningfully, with just a hint of a smile.

Sara took it without looking at it, and spooned potatoes on top of her fruit salad while she kept her eyes on Rennie. ". . . pink I think. PINK I THINK! Funny, huh? Mrs. Rampling, my English teacher, said I have an ear for poetry, but I don't know. Maybe. I mean I just naturally make up funny little rhymes like that, all the time. My REAL passion, next to modern dance of course, is trombone. I have two—a tenor trombone and one with an F trigger that plays lower. And I JUST ADORE rock music of any kind. I may be a singer with this friend of mine's big brother's band when I get a little older. I heard your stereo playing upstairs, and I just thought . . ."

I glanced over to see Rennie frowning out the window, ignoring Sara completely. I'd never seen anybody ignore Sara before.

"You ought to chase that little kid out of your old

37

house over there," Rennie suddenly said in that fast, high voice of his, turning toward Grandpa. "He's liable to fall through the floor and sue the pants off you."

"What kid?" Sara piped, bouncing in her chair to look out the window over Wade's shoulder. "I don't see any . . ."

"Hey, shut up a second, okay? I wasn't talking to you!" Rennie glared angrily at Sara. She slumped down in her chair, her mouth open and moving like a guppy's and her beautiful eyes wide as quarters and misty like she was thinking about crying.

Everybody stopped eating at Rennie's outburst, and I drew in my breath in surprise—nobody talked to Sara that way. In fact, nobody in my family often used words as harsh as "shut up" to anyone, period. But especially not to Sara.

"Oren!" Grandpa stared at Rennie, his jaw muscles working and his fists clenched on the table in front of him. Then his eyes flickered quickly to Gram, who put a finger to her lips, as if warning him. "At this table, we'll have manners," Grandpa finished, a little more softly. "Is that understood?"

"Oh, sure, I understand that just fine and dandy. I'm not stupid, you know, in spite of what my mother told you."

Rennie scraped his chair back, smiling sarcastically, threw his napkin on his plate, and shook his head as he stalked from the room.

Grandpa stood up too, his square face dark pink and angry, his big, hairy knuckles digging into the tablecloth.

"You'll ask to be excused before you leave your grandmother's table, boy!"

"No, Franklin. Please, just let him be," Gram whispered quickly, raising a hand toward Grandpa across the table.

Grandpa stood silent then, but so red in the face I was afraid he might explode. The front screen door slammed shut behind Rennie. Luther moaned a little under the table, asking for food, and Wade quickly slipped him something.

Then everybody was totally quiet again, afraid even to chew.

"Well, Elijah, shouldn't we be getting back to sharpening those mower blades?" Wade finally asked after a couple of minutes, his voice just slightly too cheerful.

Elijah quickly nodded, looking relieved. "Gram? Would you excuse us?"

"Surely, surely, go, go," Gram said, waving a hand in the air. She sounded distracted, and was looking out the window as she spoke, frowning toward the old house. "Just everyone remember—tomorrow we all go to decorate the graves for Memorial Day. Don't anyone wander so far in the morning that I can't fetch you when I need you."

I glanced toward Sara—her chin was quivering.

And though I remember being terribly shocked at myself at the time, a little part of me was glad.

Right before bed I went outside again, just to ramble. There wasn't a moon that night, and the clover fields were filled with millions of fireflies. I had my penlight with me, and hoped to match the signal of one of the firefly species so that some of them would mistake my light for theirs and signal me back. I knew from my reading that should work, but it was always too light in the city to try it. Here, though, it was so dark it was hard to tell where the stars ended and the fireflies began.

Beneath the apricot trees a shadow moved, and squinting, I recognized Elijah, standing exactly where I'd first seen him that afternoon.

"Tory!" he whisper-called, and I walked in his direction.

"Don't you love it out here at night?" I asked as I got near him. "Everything seems so alive—the stars, the wind, the . . ."

"Tory, listen, when we were out here this afternoon did you see anything like what Oren was talking about? In the old house? A . . . a kid, in the window?"

"What?" The wind came up, and I suddenly felt shivery. "No, of course not. That old house has been locked up and boarded for years . . . hasn't it?"

"Sure," Elijah answered after a few seconds. "It must have been my . . . I mean Oren's imagination."

Chapter 5

Gram had given Elijah and Rennie the two slope-ceilinged bedrooms upstairs. She assigned Sara and me to the big bedroom downstairs, next to the parlor and across the hall from where she and Grandpa slept. This was disappointing in a way—I would much rather have had the third little room upstairs, the one tucked under the eaves and used as a storage room. But I hated to complain, and besides—I had a plan. I figured if I could get Grandpa to let me set up my field laboratory in a vacant corner of one of the storage sheds, maybe later I could put a sleeping bag out there. Then when I wanted to I could sleep out there and get up before dawn to do my collecting and categorizing.

My first priority, then, was talking to Grandpa about space for my lab. I got up before light that first morning to try and catch him, but when I went into the kitchen, coffee cups and cereal bowls were stacked in the sink and he and Elijah were already gone.

Holding the screen door carefully so it wouldn't let out its usual screech, I crept onto the porch, then out into the yard.

The sky was a murky gray, but the horizon in the east was raw pink, almost red. The birds were out in force, all talking at once, and the grass was soaked and glistening with heavy dew and with spiderwebs.

I began to hear the dull, heavy, faraway sounds of other farms waking up—chutes and gates opening and closing, metal scraping against metal, cows mooing hungrily and impatiently. Dogs in the distance were baying their lungs out, and the coyotes hiding in the fencerows answered, their whines higher and somehow more lonely and wild than the cries of the dogs. I remembered one Christmas, here at the farm, when I'd seen a coyote slink close enough to the barn to steal one of Gram's chickens that had wandered back into the apricot orchard. The coyote loped across the frozen meadows with the chicken still flapping in its mouth. Red, red blood spotted the white snow.

I shivered and smiled, remembering. The world was full of danger and possibilities, especially at dawn. I loved dawn, and always had. I loved the day's extremes—dark night, and dawn.

My foot suddenly throbbed—I'd stepped on a thorn from the rambling roses that climbed up one side of the cow barn. As I leaned against the rough oak of the barn rubbing the sore place, I realized that I'd pulled on a t-shirt and jeans when I'd gone to the kitchen to find Grandpa, but I had been in such a hurry that I

42

hadn't put on my shoes. I was wandering pretty far from the house still barefoot, and decided to go back to get something on my feet.

But at that moment the orange sun popped like a bubble from the clover field and revealed huge monsters rising slowly from the stubble of last year's corn in the pasture ahead of me. Catching my breath, I walked toward them, fascinated, trying to clear the sun's dazzle from my eyes.

"Hey there!" Elijah threw up a long arm and waved, then cupped his hands around his mouth. "Come to help with chores?"

Grandpa turned toward me too then, and the sun rose higher, over the horizon, throwing a blanket of that golden yellow light gently over the fields, and over the three of us.

"Can I?" I called eagerly.

And Grandpa waved for me to join them where they stood in that field of what turned out to be huge pigs, pigs that would grow to be five-hundred-pounders, big as baby hippos, before they were sold at market that next fall.

"Go get you some boots on first, though," he called.

And that's how it happened that from that first morning on I started getting up at 4:30 every morning and dressing in some of the rubber boots and coveralls that hung in the mud room to help with the feeding and milking. The three of us—Elijah, Grandpa, and I—shared a secret morning life. Only we knew that the pigs were primeval beasts, surfacing each morning. Only we heard those first dawn sounds crossing the fields, mysterious and distant as signals from outer space. And only we had seen the huge oak farm buildings floating weightlessly in the cold night mist rising from the fields.

As we trudged back to the house after cleaning up the milking equipment, Grandpa put an arm around my shoulders. I asked him then about space for my science lab, and he chuckled and told me I could have the entire hayloft above the cow barn.

Usually Grandpa and Elijah would have gone on to the fields when the morning chores were done, but it was Memorial Day and Gram had warned we were all expected to stick close to the house, and to get ready to decorate the graves.

When we came into the kitchen, she had the round oak table covered with coffee cans—cans she must have been saving all year—and was busily covering each of them with aluminum foil.

"Well, holler when you're about ready to go," Grandpa said impatiently, taking his pipe from his shirt pocket and his Prince Edward tobacco can from the back pocket of his overalls. "Elijah and I had best get a little done in the barn, till the others see fit to terminate their beauty sleep."

Grandpa had no patience with people who stayed in bed all day, which to him meant after six o'clock in the morning. He gave me a quick wink as he turned to go back outside, and I felt proud and as happy as I could ever remember feeling.

"Now, you two leave time to shower and dress in your Sunday clothes!" Gram called after him. "You hear me, Franklin?"

Grandpa raised a hand to say he did, and the two of them disappeared down the grassy path to the huge machinery shed where the two big tractors and the combine were kept.

"Here, honey." Gram, probably sensing that I felt left out, took a big, flat-bottomed wicker basket from the pantry and handed it to me. "Don't go inside the old place, of course, but go on down the gravel road to the yard around the old house and pick any irises and roses and peonies you can find that are fresh and pretty, will you?" She looked out the east window as she began molding another piece of foil to another can, and her light blue eyes became misty. "Not too many flowers will grow around there anymore, what with all the weeds and such. But I think it's important to decorate my grandmother's grave with flowers that spread wild from her own kitchen garden."

I decided to cut across the fields instead of taking the gravel road the half-mile or so to the old house. I went out the kitchen door, ran, heels echoing on the wood, around the three turns of the wraparound porch, and jumped down into the tall grass on the side of the house by the apricot orchard.

Something tore at my sleeve as I jumped—some-

45

thing on the last of the six pillars. I climbed back on the porch to look closely.

Nails—every couple of feet somebody had hammered a long, thick nail, really more of a spike, into the graceful rounded wood of the pillar. The nails formed a sort of . . .

". . . ladder," I whispered out loud. Rennie had made himself a ladder from his room to the ground.

The delicate wood was cracking a little around a couple of the nails, and the sight caught at my stomach. Elijah could repair a broken screen, but not this. The damage was done.

Stunned at Rennie's thoughtlessness, I straightened up and as I did my eyes brushed across the old house in the distance. And I almost forgot to keep breathing because I saw, or thought I saw, somebody in the round attic window.

It seemed to be a small boy. He had his left hand raised, almost as if he was signaling me across the wide green clover fields between us.

I can't remember feeling worried or scared.

I just remember that I understood I shouldn't take my eyes from him. Afraid even to blink, I left the yard, tore through the apricot orchard, and started running full speed through the clover with my eyes on that attic window. I turned one or the other of my ankles every few yards on the uneven, gopher-holed ground, but still I never took my eyes from the window, not for a second.

As I got closer, the boy got clearer. He had tangled

brown hair and was waving slowly, rhythmically, opening and closing his left hand like little kids do before they discover they're supposed to move their whole arm. There was something strange about him, I thought. He was too solemn. Or too . . . something. Expressionless? Colorless? But maybe any strangeness was just caused by the glare of the glass, or the decades of dust caking the old window.

At Moccasin Creek, within yards of where the fields ended and the overgrown lawn of the old house began, I had to look down from the window, to figure out a way to cross the shallow water.

I spotted four flat stones, hurried to them, and hopped across.

Then I jerked my head up, eagerly sought and quickly focused on the window again.

But the boy was gone.

Chapter 6

Most of the floors in the old house were rotted out in places and soft with decay in others, which was one of the main reasons Grandpa had boarded the house up. The boy might just now have fallen through the rotten attic floor! Another awful thought crowded with that one in my mind. Grandpa had mentioned once that the beams overhead in the attic were partly rotted away from rain coming through the big holes in the roof. One of those beams might have fallen on the little boy, and . . .

"Stay right where you are!" I yelled in panic, dropping the basket. "I'm coming, so just don't try to move, okay?"

There was no answer, just the rustling of the leaves as a little breeze stirred the brambles where the overgrown lawn began a hundred yards or so in front of me.

I ran full-speed toward the lawn. The house loomed inside its bramble barrier, weathered to a bare gray, not an inch of paint left on it. I couldn't find an entrance through the high, thorny brambles, and ran along the edge of the property, looking for some sort of opening. The other round attic window, the one on the north side and not visible from Gram's house, came into view, and I had the creepy impression that the house itself was watching me from those two window eyes.

I gave up on finding an opening. Flailing with my arms and legs, trying to ignore the pain of the brambles and wild rose branches tearing at me, I shoved on through the first and thickest wall of overgrowth, and finally stood in the yard itself, which was less overgrown but crisscrossed with fallen trees and layers of dead leaves.

Something skittered through the thick groundcover, into the tall elm fencerow on my right. My heart was suddenly slamming, slamming, so I bent over with my hands on my knees and gulped several breaths of humid, decay-smelling air. The air was suffocatingly wet and hot, like steam was rising from the house itself, or the earth below it.

"I'm coming, okay? Now just don't move!" I listened, expecting the boy to respond or expecting to hear him cry out or whimper, or at least breathe. But now even the trees were silent. There was no sound. Not even the sound of locusts. There were always locusts in Illinois in summer, and the absence of their droning chant was maybe the scariest thing of all.

Dodging and kicking through the weeds and over

fallen trees, I finally reached the small stone front porch, which had partly caved in to the basement. I looked down and saw the glint of water, and thought I also saw things moving in it, leaving "V's" in their wake. Swallowing hard, I looked up at the old screen door with its delicately carved wooden frame. It was hanging in pieces by one hinge. The heavy oak inside door was locked, and boarded. No one could possibly have gotten through.

I ran around the side of the house to the other porch, this one curved and set between an angle of two rooms. There were two doors here, but when I jerked on the knobs I found that both were locked as tightly as the front door had been.

"How'd you get into the house?" I screamed to the boy, blood pounding in my ears. "Answer me so I can help get you out!"

But no answer came through that eerie vacuum of quiet.

Sobbing and panting, I staggered around the entire foundation of the house, searching in panic for a crack somewhere large enough for a boy to crawl through.

Nothing.

I reeled backwards, and looked over my head. Spindly, nearly leafless trees grew close to the house on all sides. Could he have climbed one of them and entered the house through an upstairs window or a hole in the roof? Possibly, but what little boy would have, or could have, done that? After all, he hadn't looked over five years old, at the most.

I didn't think I could climb up one of those trees and onto the roof, even to help him. And that thought of my own physical weakness made me feel almost sick to my stomach.

"Listen to me! I'm going to run home and get some help!" I wiped sweat and dirt from my forehead with my shaking hand wrapped in my t-shirt bottom. "I'll be back with some grown-ups!"

And then I ran—through the brambles, out of that nightmarish damp heat and into the cool morning sunshine, through the clover and then across the creek without bothering to use the rocks, through the pockmocked soil under the clover again, tripping and falling to one knee over and over and getting up and running blindly on, until finally I neared the apricot orchard, and suddenly Elijah was running to meet me.

"Hey, Tory! Hey, what happened? Calm down—it's okay, it's okay."

He held me by both shoulders, and I felt my knees trying to collapse. But I jerked away, grabbed his arm, and tried to pull him back through the field with me. "Come on, Elijah! You have to help him. Now!"

"Hey, what's going on? Did you see that kid?" Rennie was calling to us from the porch roof outside his escape window, his hands cupped around his mouth like a megaphone.

"Yes! He's trapped in the house, and I couldn't get to him!" Frustrated and hysterical, I rubbed my eyes with my dirty palms. "Come on, you guys! You're wasting time!"

Rennie slid to the edge of the house, and jumped down into the irises I'd straightened yesterday. He came toward us—infuriatingly calmly, slowly, his arms folded across his chest and his frowning eyes on the old house in the distance.

Just then, Gram and Sara appeared around the edge of the house near the flower gardens, carrying baskets of irises and daffodils and roses.

"Gram!" I ran toward her. "There's a little boy, trapped! Probably the boy Rennie was trying to tell us about at dinner last night, the one who's been messing around in the old house. I called and called, but he didn't come out, and I think he fell or something because . . . because, oh, he didn't even answer me! He didn't! Oh, we've got to . . ."

But something in her eyes stopped me cold.

"Victoria, now come into the house," she said softly, calmly, almost chanting the words. "And, boys, you too. Sara and I will just put these flowers in the containers we've made, and meanwhile it's time you all three showered and dressed to go to the cemetery."

"But, Gram," Elijah interrupted. "Shouldn't we go check out . . ."

"Shhh, now. Shhhh," she said, waving one hand lightly through the air like she was waving away a pesky fly. "There's nothing there to pay any mind to. Nothing at all. Nothing."

Rennie openly stared at her, his hands on his hips and his mouth gaping open. Elijah looked at her too, then looked at the ground, the muscles in his jaws working.

"But . . . but, Gram," I said again, though my voice now sounded stringy and weak to me. "I know I . . . saw him. Trapped."

"What you saw was nothing, child," she repeated, her voice lullaby gentle. "Come on into the house now, all of you."

She turned, and Sara took her hand and went with her, chattering about the bouquets they were going to make.

The three of us followed slowly behind them. From the machine shed came a clanking, the sound of machinery being repaired.

"I'll get Wade and we'll check it out," Elijah whispered when we'd almost reached the kitchen door, then took off at a run.

"No way, man," Rennie muttered. "You're not cutting out without me!"

He ran after Elijah, and before I could let myself wonder whether I should or not, I followed him.

Elijah crouched beside the cultivator and, bending toward where Wade worked, explained what I'd seen at the old house. But Wade shocked us by not being any more willing than Gram had been to rush to the rescue of the boy.

"Well, I tell you what. What you all saw was a mirage," he said, pronouncing it "mere age." His voice from under the cultivator seemed slow and almost cautious, as though he was being careful to choose each word right. "It's been seen by others before you kids, and as you say, it looks mighty real. But it's a mirage all the same, like they got out on the desert. Starts as a reflection of a certain elm tree with a skinny branch growing out from the side, and when the wind blows just right that old, old glass distorts the reflection and makes it look mighty like a boy, waving his left hand at folks."

"But, Wade," I interrupted impatiently, "why does Gram act so weird when we mention it?"

After a few seconds, Wade scooted out, a wrench in one hand and a big red handkerchief in the other, wiping his forehead.

"I reckon you'll sometime have to ask HER about that," he said, without meeting any of our eyes.

"Oh, right," Rennie murmured with a sarcastic laugh, shaking his head.

I heard a sound, and looked toward the bright rectangle of light outside the wide machine shed door. Gram and Sara were coming out the screen kitchen door, carrying Gram's foil-covered cans, now filled with bright flowers, toward the car.

"We'd better get inside and get cleaned up," I said with a sigh, and Elijah nodded. Rennie followed us toward the door, scuffing his feet through the dust, and Wade shoved himself back under the cultivator. Luther hurried over from where he'd been lying in the corner and stuck his nose against the fringe of bright orange hair sticking out near the cultivator's back wheel. Convinced it was Wade, he went back to the corner, lay down, and immediately started snoring again.

"But just one thing," Wade said softly, and we all three stopped in our tracks and strained to hear. "Uh, if'n you ask your grandmother what she thinks about that window in that old house, don't you expect to get a quick and easy answer from her. And if she gives you one, don't you expect it to be the entire truth of the matter. No, nothin' quick and easy is like to be the entire truth a'tall."

I think we all three would have liked to ask what he meant by that. After all, his own explanation—a mirage—had been quick and easy. But Gram had one hand to her eyes and was scanning the yard for us, and after a couple of minutes of silence it was pretty obvious Wade had said all he was going to say.

"Thanks, Wade," Elijah finally said, and the three of us headed reluctantly for the house.

Chapter 7

"**W**ow, it looks like people are having a huge picnic here!" Sara observed as Grandpa pulled the station wagon into one of the little grassy lanes that wound through McKendree Chapel Cemetery.

I elbowed her slightly, thinking that was sort of disrespectful, but Gram turned toward us from her place between Elijah and Grandpa in the front seat and smiled. "Everybody from the whole county comes out here on Memorial Day to decorate the graves of their ancestors and to visit with old friends. Everybody will be back for a real picnic here this August, though—the Chapel Picnic, our annual fund-raiser to pay for the cemetery's upkeep."

Grandpa edged his huge old Buick slowly between rows of other cars—it seemed strange to see all the little lanes crowded like this, when the cemetery was usually totally deserted when you drove by. But even stranger were the lawn chairs—people had brought them so they could cluster around family headstones, sitting and talking to other family members and neighbors.

"If I'm buried out here when I die, be sure to bring me a chicken leg and a can of Pepsi on Memorial Day instead of any stupid flowers," Rennie said. "Just hold that leg out and I'll raise up a bony hand to grab it."

Sara giggled, but everybody else seemed a little uneasy with his joke.

"On second thought, make that two chicken legs," he murmured, and, looking bored, he slumped further in his seat. "And be sure to put my stereo beside me when you plant me, with a good selection of records nearby."

"All right, all right, that's enough, Oren," Grandpa said, the back of his neck pink under where his felt hat pushed down the long white curls of his hair.

Grandpa maneuvered the car into a small parking spot off the lane, and we all six walked together around the family graves, putting down foil-covered cans of flowers while Gram told us stories about our ancestors.

"Uncle Harley here was a great one for practical jokes," she said, stooping to brush cedar needles from Uncle Harley's tombstone. "One April Fools' Day we'd all just sat down for dinner together, when he announces that the big east chimney is falling down! Your granddad got up and rushed to the window so quick he caught the edge of the dinner table with his knee and tilted it clear over! My, but we had a mess!"

"Were you mad, Grandpa?" Sara asked, stooping to put one of her cans of flowers on the grave.

"Just at myself," Grandpa said, chuckling. "By then I should have known it was just Harley fooling me. My brother caught me unawares many times like that over the years."

Gram and Grandpa kept stopping to chat with neighbors and friends. Once when they were deep in conversation with another couple, Rennie slipped behind a cedar tree, jerked off his tie and crammed it in his pocket, and unbuttoned his top shirt button.

He put a finger to his lips when he saw I'd spotted him.

"I've had enough of this circus," he whispered through the prickly branches between us. "Tell them I'll see them at home."

"But . . ."

"I'm leaving too," Elijah said, overhearing Rennie and turning to walk back to us. "Wade really needs help fixing the cultivator."

Rennie took off, running in the direction of Chapel Hill Ridge, and Elijah followed, staying a careful few yards behind.

"Elijah doesn't like Rennie much," Sara observed, more or less echoing my thoughts with her usual outspoken breeziness. "But he should. I do. I like Rennie a bunch, even if he did sort of yell at me last night. Elijah's probably just super jealous."

"Of what?" I asked. Some of Sara's ideas took me totally by surprise, especially because they so often turned out to be right.

She shrugged as if it were obvious. "Jealous of Rennie's street smarts. Rennie is so cool. And he has tons of cherrysma. Elijah's just a plain farm kid."

"Charisma," I automatically corrected. "Not 'cherry'—it's 'chari,' like with a 'k.' "

"So you noticed he had it too, huh?" she said with a smug little smile, then tossed her dark hair over her shoulder and skipped on ahead to rejoin Gram and Grandpa.

As I watched her run up and take Gram's hand it suddenly dawned on me that the boys weren't going home at all. They were going to use this time while Gram and Grandpa were preoccupied to go creeping around the old house, to find the waving boy! I hit the side of my head with my palm just like they do in slapstick movies—how could I have been so dumb?

I felt really left out, insulted and hurt. After all, he was MY boy! I'd seen him the closest up, and probably for the longest time. Rennie and Elijah probably just didn't think I could keep up with them as they ran the mile and a half to the old house, then thrashed their way through the overgrown lane.

Again, I was left standing alone and unchosen by the team captains. I looked at Gram and Grandpa and Sara, a few yards away. Gram had her arm around Sara's shoulders, and Sara was beaming prettily while Gram introduced her to some friends. I could tell from my sister's self-assured smile that Gram was telling those people about all of Sara's numerous talents and abilities.

Why should I go stand gawkily by my beautiful

little sister while she was reveling in attention? Gram would just fish desperately around for some way to brag about me to keep it even.

And why should I have to be Elijah and Rennie's designated excuse-giver? The unadventurous one left behind the other, cooler kids to explain things to the adults?

"Well, this isn't Milwaukee and this time I won't," I mumbled in answer to all my mental questions. Then without a word to anyone, I took off running in the direction the boys had gone.

They were far ahead of me and seemed to bob like puppets in the shimmery heat of the dusty road. I didn't call to them to wait—I wasn't that sure I could run the whole way and I definitely didn't want to admit to them halfway there that I couldn't keep up.

Chapel Hill Ridge runs high above the surrounding fields for about a mile past the cemetery, then you go down steep McKendree Hill and take a right turn at the big forked oak tree to go on to the two houses. The boys disappeared around the oak tree turn a long time before I got there. When I reached it they were just turning into the long overgrown lane of the old ruined house.

As I leaned against the oak tree to grab a breath, the old house looked to me like a huge waiting white monster, Moby Dick or the Abominable Snowman. The partly fallen back porch, with its snaggle-teeth of hanging shingles, was a stretched pair of waiting jaws, and Elijah and Rennie were headed innocently and directly into them.

A frantic screeching racket suddenly started up directly over my head, and two tattered red-wing blackbirds half fell and half flew to the ground near my feet, fighting over something. I shuddered, my heart jumped like a caged animal in my chest, and the golden light thickened around me so much I wondered if I was going to faint. I didn't wait to find out. Instead, before I could let myself hesitate a second longer, I ran on.

Chapter 8

Elijah and Rennie had pushed back branches and torn aside vines to form a sort of tunnel through the brush crowding the lane. I looked across the fields, toward the other, safer house. The things Gram had hung to dry on the clothesline by the flower garden—aprons and overalls looking from this distance like tiny doll clothes—were somehow reassuring. Holding my breath, I stooped and hurried into the tunnel. Behind me I could hear the sounds of the birds and locusts, but ahead of me I heard nothing.

"Elijah?" I called, emerging finally into the shadowy overgrown yard. "Rennie?"

The thick vegetation seemed to absorb my voice like it absorbed the sunlight.

I walked toward the house, picking my way as I had earlier that morning over the tangled bushes and decaying ground cover. I had the weirdest sensation that what I was walking on wasn't really earth, but was something spongy that would suck me down and under the ground at any second.

"Elijah! Where are you guys! Rennie?"

And then I noticed—one of the two doors that led inside from the back porch was wide open. This morning, both had been closed, locked shut.

A sharp sound and a movement in the round attic window high above my head drew my eyes reluctantly upward. There was a hand in the window, but it wasn't waving. It was clawing, spiderlike, at the glass. Its nails screeched as it slid and climbed, then slid again. While I watched, the other hand appeared, pulling slowly upward on a thick, knotted rope. And then a head emerged above the sill—a head with the other end of the rope around its neck, its tongue hanging out, its blue eyes rolling wildly in their sockets . . .

"TRICK OR TREAT, SMELL MY FEET!" the head suddenly yelled down at me, flipping its tongue in and out a few times. Then Rennie broke into wild laughter. "I got you! Admit it, Tory, I got you!"

"Oh, right, Rennie, I'm so sure I didn't know that was you up there!" I called to him.

But I had to hurry forward and sit on the cool, solid stone of the porch stairs for a few seconds before I could trust my legs to carry me on into the house.

The house smelled like decaying leaves inside. A lot of the plaster had fallen off the ceilings, exposing heavy beams, and ivy crawled from the holes in the floors and up the walls like snakes. My shoulder rubbed against the wooden door to the parlor and came away damp, and chilly. I touched that wood again with my fingertips—there were beads of condensation clinging to it, round and solid as tiny ladybugs.

When I got to the front hallway and reached the winding staircase that led upstairs, Elijah was coming down to meet me.

"Watch your step," he warned. "The stairs are weird—they move around a little when you step on them. And the floors upstairs are almost nonexistent."

The stairs were weird all right—they echoed your footsteps, and they were shaped like little individual boxes.

"Have you been inside this house before?" I asked him.

He shook his head. "Never. Ever since I can remember Grandpa has warned me to stay out of it, that it's liable to . . ."

". . . fall down at any minute. I know, he's always told Sara and me the same thing. Uh, why are we whispering?"

We both laughed at ourselves, but nervously.

"There's a small hallway and three bedrooms up here," Elijah said in a louder, too-normal voice as he reached the top step. "The two attic gables are over the two bedrooms on the west and north side, and you can see the round attic windows through the ceilings. Or what used to be the ceilings."

Standing in the little hallway, you could look in all three bedrooms just by slightly moving your head. Elijah went into the room on the right. I stood looking into the north room, the one directly in front of me. I didn't like the fact that Rennie was being so quiet. Obviously he was hiding somewhere, ready to spring another hilarious surprise, and until he did I planned to remain in the hall, where I could see him no matter which room he happened to be in when he did the springing.

And that's when something moved in the room on my left. I saw it with my peripheral vision—it seemed to start from inside the open cubbyhole of a closet. It moved quickly across the room, and disappeared into the wall on the east side. It was about as high as my waist, and dark, greenish or grayish. I had the clear impression that it didn't want to be seen, had been hiding and waiting since the boys had come up here for its chance to leave undetected before any of us entered that room.

It moved so quickly that by the time I jerked my head in its direction, it was gone.

"Aaaarghhh! Heeeeelp!" I almost jumped out of my skin at Rennie's scream, and Elijah and I both ran into the middle room and looked high above our heads to see him balanced on one of the highest roof beams, teetering on one foot, windmilling his arms.

He was right on the brink of falling fifteen feet or so to the floor where Elijah and I stood; then he would surely crash on through the rotten ceiling lathe and into the room below us. My mind barely had time to comprehend the fact that the fall might quite possibly kill him, when he quit teetering, put his hands on his hips nonchalantly, and crossed the toe of one foot over the other foot.

He stood on that beam for all the world like he was waiting, bored, for the school bus.

"Oh, man," Elijah moaned, shaking his head. I knew he wouldn't admit it in a million years, but Rennie had really scared him.

Rennie laughed. "Relax! My dad and I climb rocks all the time, in Colorado and places. We walk along rims across the tops of cliffs that make this beam seem a mile wide."

He extended his arms and walked quickly and effortlessly the rest of the distance along the narrow beam, then swung easily off, caught the beam with his hands, dangled, then jumped down to one of the few remaining intact attic floorboards.

"Your weight could have broken that old beam, you know," Elijah said quietly but, I could tell, angrily. "In fact, it's just pure luck it didn't."

"Hey, lighten up, will you, cousin? You're not my boss. Or even my friend, for that matter."

Rennie swung by his arms from the floor joist down through where the ceiling used to be. His feet hung maybe five feet from the floor to the middle room, and he let go and jumped down right beside Elijah.

"Yeah, well, at the rate you're going your friends will be coming to your funeral before the summer's over," Elijah murmured.

"What do you care, man?" Rennie demanded, flexing his fingers as he walked toward the door. "What's it to you, anyhow? Just live your safe little farmboy life, but me—I'm pushing the envelope this summer! I'm going for it! Just buck your hay bales and milk your cows, man, 'cause you'll never in your life even understand what I'm talking about."

Elijah turned to the window, his shoulders stiff.

"See you back at home sweet home, cousins," Rennie snickered as he passed me in the hall and rode the bannister down the stairway.

A few seconds later we heard his feet pounding on the porch floor, and seconds after that we saw him duck into the brush tunnel.

"Elijah?" I said, and swallowed hard. "Don't let him get to you. Okay?"

Elijah was staring out the dirt-streaked window, watching Rennie jog down the lane. When I went closer to him, I was really surprised by the look on his face. I guess I'd expected him to look disgusted with Rennie's showing off. But instead he looked almost dazed, or hypnotized, and I remembered Sara's off-the-wall comment about him envying Rennie's "cherrysma."

"Elijah, listen. I . . . I thought I saw something really strange just now. Something sort of . . . sort of creepy."

It took him just a half-second longer than I thought it would to turn from Rennie to me. "Strange?" he asked.

"In here." I waited for him to join me in the hall before I had the courage to look again into the left bedroom. "Something moved, and then just sort of . . . disappeared. Into the . . . wall."

The sun was pouring that golden light through both windows in the left bedroom, and the old torn wallpaper, paper once new and patterned with cheerful yellow roses, looked innocent and normal.

"Or maybe Wade's right," I said with a sigh. "Maybe I saw shadows, from the trees outside. Maybe it's all a mirage."

"Yeah, maybe," Elijah said a minute later.

But he didn't really sound convinced.

Chapter 9

When Elijah and I got home, Grandpa's station wagon was back in the driveway, and another car—a long white Ford with a beige top was parked right behind it.

"Oh, no," Elijah murmured, obviously recognizing the car. He loped toward the machinery shed. "I'm out of here."

"Elijah!"

"Gotta help with the cultivator!" he called back over his shoulder. "Besides, she already gave me one!"

She? One what?

"Great," I muttered, hoping Rennie had already caught the brunt of the scolding we all three deserved for running away from the cemetery.

I braced myself as I pulled open the screen door, but Gram and Sara and a visitor were sitting at the kitchen table drinking iced tea, and they all turned my way, smiling broadly.

"Well, there you finally are!" Gram said. "Victoria, this is my dearest friend in the world, Tillie Myerson. And, Tillie, this is Victoria, my elder granddaughter."

"She brought us Bibles!" Sara chirped, holding hers up in the air toward me. "See? White ones! With zippers and everything!"

Tillie Myerson leaned over and patted Sara's hand. "Precious child," she said, smiling with her lips pursed like she was getting ready to spit, though I knew, of course, she wasn't. She definitely wasn't the spitting type. Short and round, she was dressed all in turquoise—turquoise velvet hat with a little turquoise net, turquoise dress a few sizes larger than Gram wore, shiny turquoise shoes and purse in a slightly greener shade than her dress, and little turquoise and pink flowers embroidered on her white gloves. Clear from the door I could smell her lilac toilet water, and her powder.

If she'd been an insect she would have been a rare and striking iridescent-blue beetle.

"She gives all the neighborhood kids Bibles, isn't that neat?" Sara chattered on. "Black ones for the boys, white ones for the girls. I plan on keeping mine forever and ever and reading at least one or two chapters a day. At least. And I'll probably memorize bunches of things because my teachers say I have a real knack for memorization. Like, for instance, in cheerleading routines, the others have to try real hard to memorize the moves, but I . . ."

"Precious child," Tillie Myerson said again, this time patting Sara's hand in a no-nonsense way that was more like a slap. She stood up, and fished for a second in her handbag—which I suddenly noticed was huge like a suitcase. With a flourish, she handed me my Bible. "May it prove a blessing to you, dear."

"Thank you," I said, tongue-tied. I already had a Bible, and so did Sara. We'd had them for years, since we were little kids.

Mrs. Myerson was moving toward the door, chit-chatting with Gram, her heels clacking on the linoleum like beetle feet.

I heard my voice. "Gram, uh, has she met . . . Oren?"

Gram looked from me to Mrs. Myerson, then back to me, then to Mrs. Myerson. She swallowed, gulped really. It was one of the few times I'd ever seen her at a loss for words.

"Oren is my other cousin, besides Elijah, whom I understand you've already met," I said to Mrs. Myerson, smiling ultra-politely. "I'm sure Oren would just love to meet you. If you'll excuse me, I'll just run upstairs and get him."

This would teach Rennie to play practical jokes on us.

I ran upstairs and hammered on Rennie's door. "Gram says you have to come down, into the kitchen," I whispered quickly when he finally heard me knocking over the noise of his stereo and opened the door a crack.

Rolling his eyes and with a dramatic sigh, he squeezed past me and thumped on sullenly down the stairs.

What was coming over me? At home I would never have had the nerve to do something like this to someone like him. I pushed my back against the wall and slid to the floor, covering my mouth as I sat huddled there, giggling my head off.

Several minutes later Rennie came tramping back upstairs. I felt my neck burning, and figured I'd have to explain myself, but I didn't because he had his new black Bible open and was holding it sideways, frowning at a picture in it as he walked. He didn't even seem to notice me still sitting there.

After we'd eaten lunch that day and the kitchen was cleaned up, everyone scattered. Grandpa lay down outside in the hammock for a nap. Rennie jogged off to who knew where. Elijah and Wade went back out to the machine shed. Sara went to sit by the goldfish pond, and from our bedroom window I watched her turning the pages of her white Bible. I wanted to begin setting my field lab up in the hayloft, but I couldn't get the old house and the waving boy out of my mind.

Sara saw me watching her out the window and jumped up from the big limestone rock, holding up her open Bible. "Look at this, Victoria! Births! Deaths! Marriages! There's a whole section between the Old Testament and the New Testament for recording stuff, and it's got these neat flower decorations on each page! I can't wait to get started filling in these pages. Cool, huh?''

I felt irritated with her—why couldn't she play along and start calling me Tory, at least while we were here at the farm?

"I guess," I murmured unenthusiastically. "But you don't have anything to write about. There hasn't been a birth or a death or a marriage in our family during your entire lifetime."

She closed the Bible, put it in her lap, and stretched her fingers across it protectively. "Well, not everyone just sticks every dead thing they find in a dumb collecting box, like you do," she told me.

I had my choice of asking what in the world she was talking about or turning away from the window, so I turned away from the window, picked up my collecting box, and headed outside.

But as I entered the kitchen, I noticed Gram sitting in her rocker by the east window, a flyswatter in one hand and a cardboard fan with a tractor advertisement on it in the other. The old silver Eskimo fan squealed noisily as it moved hot, listless air from its place on top of the refrigerator.

She was looking out the window, toward the apricot trees. Toward the old house beyond them? She turned when she heard me, and acted flustered to be caught resting.

"My, my, Victoria Ann, it's surely turned out to be a scorcher, hasn't it? Just one more minute of cooling off here, and I need to be getting out to pick those green beans. They'll be withering in the heat for sure.''

So quickly I surprised myself, I put down my collecting box, darted across the room, grabbed one of the oak dining chairs, and pulled it over near her. I straddled it, eagerly peering at her over the backrest.

"Gram, will you tell me about the old house?" I asked in a rush. "Please, please, please? About when it was built and who was born in it and lived in it and . . . and if anybody died in it. Stuff like that? Then I'll go out and pick the beans for you. Please?''

She was startled, I know, by my intense interest. She smiled a tiny smile, but didn't answer. I hopped my chair forward a little farther, so my knee was touching hers and she was pretty much blocked from getting up. "Please, Gram?''

She chuckled and patted my leg. "I'm not so much of a storyteller, Victoria. I'm afraid I'd bore you stiff.''

She looked back out the window. My heart pounded.

"I know the old house was built by your grandparents, which would be my great-great-grandparents,'' I prodded. "And I know they had six children.''

Her eyes grew misty behind her glasses as she slowly shifted her gaze from the house to me again. Then she cleared her throat, took off her glasses, and wiped them on her apron.

She took a long breath, looking down at the glasses in her lap but not moving to put them back on.

"Seven," she corrected, her voice gentle, quiet, gravelly. "My grandparents had seven children, not six. But . . . but perhaps you've never heard tell of their firstborn, little Americus."

Chapter 10

"**M**y pretty, red-haired grandmother was Marcella McNeill," she began, "and her husband was Thomas McNeill, though everyone knew him as 'Neilly.'

"All of their parents had come to Pennsylvania from Ireland. And maybe Marcella and Neilly inherited their wanderlust, because in 1842, the year after they were married, they set out on their own journey, every bit as daring as crossing the Atlantic. They were bound for the fabled Land of Milk and Honey, for the place known as Oregon, far across the Rocky Mountains."

I'd heard this part of the story before, and closed my eyes to better imagine Marcella and Thomas in their Conestoga wagon, blue on the bottom and red along the sides, six horses pulling it over rutted trails.

"As they traveled from Pennsylvania to Missouri, where they'd join others bound westward on the Oregon Trail, they stopped a great many times to say a great many good-byes to relatives and friends. My, my, yes—they said good-byes upon good-byes. And they weren't halfhearted good-byes, but were forever good-byes, heart-wrenching good-byes. Because once they joined that train of wagons, Neilly and Marcella would be forever lost to those behind them, who might never even know if they lived or died along the way. As lost as their parents had been to their friends and families left behind in Ireland. As lost as if you and Sara were to board a starship to travel a treacherous path toward a distant galaxy."

Gram's voice trailed to a whisper and she sighed, then shook her head and laughed at herself.

"Now, Victoria, don't you let me ramble, or we'll never get those beans picked! As I was saying, Neilly and Marcella happened to hitch their wagon for just one April night right here, somewhere on this two hundred and sixty acres. And the next morning Marcella woke with the dawn light sifting through oak leaves, coming through the round canvas opening of the wagon and falling in gentle, dappled patterns on her face. When I was a little girl she told me many times how she tried to feel happy that morning, how she tried to remember that they were headed toward Paradise, toward the Land of Milk and Honey where things grew the minute the seed hit the ground like talked of in the Bible.

"But tears kept sliding down her face anyway. That's how she described it, in those words. 'Tears slid down my face, Dena Marie, through the shadows of those big oak leaves.' It was like a dam had burst inside her, from one too many good-byes being said like one too many drops of water flowing through a riverbed.

"So she woke up Neilly and said, 'Thomas, we can't go any farther. It's here we'll stay and build our home, on this Illinois side of the Mississippi River and the big mountains, where we have kin less than a day's drive away, and none further than two weeks.' And so they stayed."

I couldn't stop myself from interrupting. "I always wondered what Neilly said about not going on to Oregon. Didn't he argue or anything?"

Gram chuckled a little. "Well, Victoria, my grandfather was a strong man, but a practical one. Many's the time I heard him say if hail destroyed your corn, there was no use cursing the hail. And if a twister scattered your horses, there was nothing to do but wait for it to blow by. Your great-great-grandmother hardly weighed a hundred pounds, but she had a hurricane will, and my grandfather loved her for that as much as he loved her for the rest of her. So that very afternoon he rode into the nearest town, Mulberry Grove, and asked about buying some land to homestead. And on that land—this land, this two hundred and sixty acres—he first built a two-room cabin right down there, on the bank of Moccasin Creek. And the minute that cabin was built, he began work on a much grander place—the house across the clover there."

I squinted toward where Moccasin Creek moved

shining through thick stands of rushes and cattails. From this distance, the old house beyond the creek appeared to rise like a mist from the fields.

"Besides," Gram said, "there was probably another reason for Grandfather to decide they'd traveled far enough. The morning that they were camped here on our land was the morning Marcella told him she believed she was pregnant with their first child."

I caught my breath. No one had ever told me this part of the story before. "Americus?"

Gram nodded, and smiled in a sad way. "He was born in the cabin, on a bright October day that next fall. Grandmother never admitted it, but I believe they named him Americus because it was the name of an adventurer, a sayer of good-byes. My grandmother told me she had hoped that if he wanted to he would have the courage to reach the Land of Milk and Honey someday. I believe she had hoped to give him freedom with her milk as she rocked him by the east cabin window and watched Neilly build their house on the hill."

Gram stared out the window as though the past was arising again before her eyes from those old, old fields that stretched on all sides of us. When she talked again it was as though she was carefully describing what she was seeing.

"Farm work, clearing the new ground, left Neilly little time for the building of the house, but by the time Americus was three years old the beams and braces were up and Americus could scramble like a monkey through them, following his father as he worked. The first laughter those old boards heard was theirs. Grandmother told me she used to sit by the cabin, watching them up on the hill, smiling as she shelled peas or mended clothes."

I smiled too, imagining. But when I glanced at Gram her eyes were misty and her voice grew softer. I felt myself straining forward to hear so hard that the wooden rungs of the chair pressed into me. Later I noticed deep red marks along the insides of my arms.

"It was a warm day in September. Neilly was working on the rafters of the house, and Americus was with him. Marcella was hanging out a wash, when a wagon pulled into the rough lane up to the cabin. It was my great-aunt Lydie—I named Elijah's mother after her. She was Marcella's sister, and she'd come for a visit clear down from Springfield with her husband, Uncle Paul, and their four children. Marcella was, of course, overjoyed to see them.

"It had been a long, hot wagon ride, and the children . . . the children scrambled out and begged to wade and splash in Moccasin Creek. In the happy confusion of greeting everyone their mother laughingly agreed it would be a good way for them to relax and cool off and would give the adults a chance to rest a little. Marcella directed them to where there was a little sandy place, a natural beach about a hundred yards downcreek from the cabin. There was little danger—they were old enough to take care, the youngest several years older than Americus.

"But . . . Americus was watching from inside the framework of the new house. As the adults settled in on the porch of the cabin to laugh and talk, and as Neilly worked noisily on the roof of the new house unaware that company had even arrived, Americus spied his older cousins wading in the creek, and ran toward them.

"He ran right toward them, though he'd been taught to stay far from the shifting, sandy banks of Moccasin Creek, which flowed harder and much wider than it does now. The oldest of the children, Violet, only saw her little cousin approaching them moments before he lost his footing on the slick rocks. The water closed quickly and fiercely over his head and carried him downstream before any of the other children could think or react. Violet . . . Violet was crying hysterically when she ran to get Marcella. She said when she saw Americus for those few seconds he was laughing out loud, his eyes on the other children and not on his balance. Laughing out loud, even as he fell."

There was a long silence, and the next voice I heard surprised me by being mine.

"He . . . he drowned."

"Yes." Gram sadly patted my knee. "Both Neilly and Marcella blamed themselves the rest of their lives. No one was ever to know why Americus, a boy who always minded, disobeyed so completely and tragically that day."

"He hadn't been around kids before," I immediately explained. It seemed so crystal clear to me. "He saw them and couldn't resist joining them. If . . . if you were a locust, and the time had come to shed your hard crust of a skin, all ordinary rules of the world around you would be suspended for the time it took you to split yourself apart and step out. Americus suddenly didn't . . . FEEL the rules."

Gram's hand quit patting and tightened on my knee. She was staring at me, a worried look in her eyes, and I laughed lightly, to reassure her.

But I myself was suddenly wondering where my strange explanation had come from.

I convinced Gram to rest, and got one of the big aluminum pans from under the sink. I took it outside to the vegetable garden, where I picked two rows of beans, then straightened up and bent backward to flex my cramped muscles. I let my eyes move to the empty round window of the old house across the fields.

Sara came running up, her white Bible in one hand and a pink crayon in the other.

"Look, look, look! I've got the Births page nearly filled up, and a good start on the Deaths!"

I didn't want to touch the Bible with my garden-dirty hands, but I bent over and squinted to read the Deaths page in the glaring sunshine.

"Uh, Sara? Wasn't 'Joan' that hamster you had several years ago? And my parakeet was 'Miss Cheepers.' 'Thistle Whiskers'?"

"All three of the deaths are pets," she said briskly,

"though I kind of had to guess at the dates they died. My hamster, your parakeet, and that mouse that was living in the kitchen that we sort of got to like before Mom finally trapped him. I had to make up a name for him—Thistle Whiskers—good, huh?"

"And here on the Births page—who are 'Dave' and 'Jasper the Prince' and . . . and 'Silverfin'?"

"Fish," Sara said, shutting the Bible with a satisfied flourish. "Some of Gram's goldfish. I estimated the dates of their births, since Grandpa told me Gram bought all the fish two years ago, at the pet store in Mulberry Grove. I made up names for the fish, too. Now, if any of them die this summer, I can add their names to the Death page. After a suitable funeral, of course."

"Of course," I said, and bent quickly back to the beans.

I couldn't wait to write Mom and Daddy about Sara's latest big idea.

"Hey, is that the kid Rennie saw?" she suddenly asked, and I jerked my eyes up and focused on the window far across the fields.

And as though he'd waited for both Sara and me to stand together looking at him, the boy was now back. He slowly raised his left hand and waved.

"Elm trees don't do that," I whispered. "Mirages don't raise their arms to wave."

"Poor boy, I'll bet he's lonely," Sara said innocently. "But now that he knows there are kids here this summer, I'll bet he'll come over and play."

Chapter 11

That night I told Elijah that Sara and I had seen the boy again. He frowned thoughtfully, but finally just shrugged.

"We start cutting hay tomorrow," he said. "I won't have time to think about much else for a couple of weeks. Let's just keep our eyes open and see what happens, or what doesn't, okay?"

I thought about telling him Gram's story about Americus, but to be honest, I wanted to keep it to myself for a while. It had seemed a special gift, from Gram to me.

And what difference would it have made? I could see Elijah was right. We'd gone over the old house with a fine-tooth comb, so what else could we do? There are times with any scientific experiment when it's best to go as far as you can, then to leave things alone to either ripen or disintegrate on their own.

I don't know if Rennie did any more snooping around the old house on his own just then or not. We weren't exactly on great speaking terms. I guess, to tell the truth, he scared me, and I avoided ever having to talk to him.

The next morning, Monday, the first day of June, I began setting up my lab in the hayloft.

The only way up to the hayloft was a rough oak ladder that was built into the wall between two of the milking stalls. Every time I stuck my head through the rough hole in the floor and entered the huge, shadowy loft, I had the sensation of emerging through a cloud to a different, more magical world. There was a thin coating of hay everywhere in the loft, and the air seemed to be always slightly swirling, carrying hayseeds and bits of dust.

The only light from the outside world came through a single house-shaped hinged window that would fold open clear to the floor. It was cut out of the rough oak the barn was built with. Closed, it left the loft practically dark as midnight even in the middle of the day.

Through that window I had a clear view of the flower garden, where Sara often puttered making an elaborate fish cemetery. I could also look over the acres of land to the old, ruined house, and, holding my breath, I scrutinized the round window probably a dozen times a day.

But through all those crisp, clear first days of June, I never once saw a trace of the waving boy.

I shared the space in the loft with three families of

barnswallows, who had their nests in deep corners of the eaves. They panicked and flew wildly as dive bombers around the ceiling the first few times they saw me, but gradually they began to stay in their nests and settled for a few warning chirps in my direction.

Grandpa had several long pieces of plywood stored up there, and he helped me bring up four sawhorses. We made two eight-foot-long tables so I could spread out my collections, and we strung a thick extension cord from downstairs so I could have a small light and my microscope on one of the tables.

It was perfect, and totally private. I could have stayed tucked away up there forever with my rocks and bugs, in my secure tower high above the world. I was like the Giant in ''Jack and the Beanstalk''— alone and safe, content in my own way with my own form of vast riches.

Until the day about a week into June when Rennie came climbing up, carelessly and selfishly as Jack himself.

''Hiding out, huh?''

''How'd you do that?'' I'd been sitting hunched over one of the tables, cleaning some small pink rocks I'd picked up in Moccasin Creek. At the sight of Rennie's round, curl-framed face in the rough loft window I jumped up so fast my stool crashed to the floor. ''How'd you get up here?''

''I told you my dad and I climb rock cliffs all the time,'' he said, pulling himself in through the window, then reeling in a long length of thick rope. ''I guess you had your nose too far in your work to even hear me throw my hook over the sill. After that, it was just a matter of holding on and climbing up the side of the barn. This rough old oak gives great traction."

Without being invited, he sauntered over to my tables, hands on his hips, eyes narrowed. After the bright sunshine outside, the darkness of the hayloft was nearly total for a while when you first came up. With one bare shoulder he wiped sweat from his eyes.

He picked up the little white box I kept my three praying mantis specimens in, lifted it close to his nose, and frowned into it. "So answer the question," he said. "Are you planning to hide out up here all summer?"

"I'm not hiding out, just working," I croaked.

He laughed. "Give me a break. Of course you're hiding, and I'll just bet you hide out with your bugs and rocks in Milwaukee too. You think it's not obvious how shy you are and how you hide and use this scientist act as a cover? You look at that little show-offy sister of yours like she's queen of the world just because she knows how to yakkety yak to people and you don't."

I was glad he was too sun-blinded to see, because I felt my mouth stretching into its idiotic embarrassment-grin.

He put the little white box down, more gently than I expected him to. "I would have helped you move this stuff up here."

"Grandpa helped me," I forced out.

He snorted a laugh. "Yeah, Grandpa would move mountains for you, or for Elijah. What do you guys do together so early in the morning, anyway?"

"Chores," I answered. "Milking, feeding, mucking out the stalls."

"The Rise and Shine Club," he said, mockingly. "For all the good little boys and girls, by invitation only." Whistling under his breath, he paced around the loft, looking things over.

I picked up the stool and began wiping it off elaborately with the tail of my t-shirt, trying to look busy and nonchalant.

"Well, gotta go," he said, finally.

He'd probably been there all of three minutes, but it seemed like an hour. He rehooked his rope to the sill, ducked out the window, and hung outside in the bright sunlight, his arms bulging with his weight as he began easing himself toward the ground.

I just stood there in the dark part of the loft and kept wiping off that stupid stool, tears burning my eyes like his words were burning my heart. "You think it's not obvious how shy you are and how you hide? You think it's not obvious . . . obvious?"

My castle walls had been breached. In a few cruel sentences Rennie had exposed me, even to myself.

I knew I could never feel perfectly hidden again.

I didn't sleep much that night. I kept running every painful word Rennie had said around and around in my mind, and finally the sky outside our bedroom window got the not-quite-dark look I knew meant dawn was somewhere near.

I slipped into my clothes and walked through the

quiet house, then through the dew in the front yard till I stood right beneath Rennie's window. I pictured myself climbing onto the porch roof and invading his territory like he had invaded mine. Though I knew I lacked the nerve to do it, the more I pictured it the better I felt.

And then I realized I'd been nervously fingering some small hard objects in my jeans pocket— a handful of tiny rocks I'd picked up at the creek the day before. I took them out and stared through the gloom at the large dark specks against my palm.

Then suddenly my arm was moving backward, backward, then forward sharply. I had actually flung that handful of gravel, hard, against Rennie's window! A few seconds later, a light came on in his room. I thought about running back around to the side of the house, but instead found myself running to the porch and forcing myself to climb up the rough ladder of nails Rennie had made in the pillar. On my knees, so scared I'd fall that I almost forgot how scared I was to do this in the first place, I made my way to his window over the shingles of the porch roof, and rapped with my knuckles.

When Rennie staggered over and raised the glass, for once, my nervous embarrassment-grin paid off. I LOOKED cheerful and maybe even mocking, instead of flustered to death.

"Hi, Rennie. I, uh, just thought I'd officially invite you to a meeting of the Rise and Shine Club."

I hung there clutching the windowsill, grinning

like a total idiot, while he stared silently back at me. Either he was too sleepy for his trademark "cool" to be in operation, or I took him so off guard he forgot to slip into it.

I expected, of course, that he'd stumble back to bed. I only wanted to expose his hypocrisy and give him a taste of his own medicine—I might be shy and hiding out, but he was self-centered and lazy.

"Uh, okay," he said instead, rubbing his face briskly with both stubby-fingered hands, and shocking me so much I nearly lost my grip on the window. "Okay, thanks. I'll be right out."

He started away, then turned back to me. "You want to go down through here?"

"Yeah, I do," I said meekly, and quickly scrambled over the sill and into his room. To this day I don't know if I could have forced myself to go backwards down that roof or not.

Another thing I don't know is how I'd expected his room to look, but I do know I was shocked. Probably I'd thought he'd have music posters around, and lots of junk on the floor. Stuff like empty pop cans and dirty clothes, stereo gadgets, tapes, and weight training equipment and comics and stuff.

But it was neat and empty. Besides his stereo on the dresser, his gym mat on the floor, and his open, but unpacked, small suitcase in the corner, the only thing in the room was a small pile of books, including the black Bible Mrs. Myerson had given him, stacked on the floor by the bed.

Chapter 12

I could tell Grandpa was surprised to see Rennie walk into the milking barn with me that first morning. He straightened from where he'd crouched to check a sore hoof on one of the cows, leaned slowly back against the shiny machine that cooled the milk, took his pipe from his overall pocket, and filled it with tobacco from his battered Prince Edward can. Grandpa never smoked in the barns, and he didn't light his pipe that morning, just stood slowly filling it as a way to take time out to comprehend the situation.

"Here, man," Elijah said, handing Rennie a feed bucket and pointing toward the grain bin over in the corner. "Fill each trough right when we lead the cow into her stall and start cleaning the udders, so she'll have her mind off the milking. Later I'll show you how to attach the milkers."

I felt relieved that Elijah had just assumed that Rennie was there to work, and hadn't asked a bunch of questions that Rennie would have probably found insulting.

"Right," Rennie mumbled, and headed for the grain bin.

That was about it for conversation that morning, but then we never talked much during the milking. The machines made too much noise, and besides, it was a time for concentration.

After that, Rennie came out to help every morning, and since three people could easily handle things, after about a week Grandpa left us alone. He'd go out with us at 4:30, get us started on things, then just sort of drift away to do other jobs, odds and ends on other parts of the farm.

With Grandpa not around to look over our shoulders, Rennie quickly substituted his own way of doing things for Grandpa's way. For instance, he'd fill both feed buckets so he'd have equal weight in both hands, then climb the thin metal fence that separated the four milking stalls. He'd then walk like a tightrope artist along that inch-wide top rail to the feed troughs. From his position above us and above the puzzled cows, he'd dump the feed in two of the four troughs, then walk back along the rail, jump off and refill the buckets at the feed bin, and climb back up the fence to repeat the process for the other two troughs.

"It works better if you wait and feed each cow separately right as we start cleaning her," Elijah complained mildly, after a couple of days of this. "That's when we need to distract them, while we get the milkers on. They shouldn't come in to full troughs of feed."

"I don't see a problem doing it this way," Rennie shot right back from where he balanced above us. "Just because it's not the way it's been done for a hundred years around here doesn't mean it's not solid."

Elijah didn't respond right away, just bent over the shovel he was using to muck out a stall. "Two of the cows are kickers," he finally said quietly. "If they come in to filled troughs, one of these days one of them is going to finish her feed too quick and get bored or irritated and hurt whoever's milking."

Rennie just shook his head and laughed a little at Elijah's reasoning, and went on doing his balancing act and filling two troughs at a time.

And, like I'd been almost sure he would, Elijah let it pass.

I can't honestly remember if I considered inviting Sara to join what Rennie called our "Rise and Shine Club." If I did consider it, I like to think that Rennie's obvious coolness toward her was what kept me from doing it, and not any reluctance on my own part.

But then about the middle of June, I came in from chores one morning to find Sara sitting cross-legged on her bed. It was about 7:30, an hour earlier than she ever got up during summer at home, or had yet here at the farm. She was bent over a bright tangle of shoelaces. She'd brought along colors to match all her outfits, and they were in a softball-sized knotted glob from being shoved around in her underwear drawer.

"Where were you, anyway?" she grumbled huskily, pushing hair from her left eye and glaring at me. "How come Grandpa lets you guys do all that cow stuff in the morning, and not me?"

"We don't just do the chores 'in the morning,' Sara. We do them before dawn. Not exactly your best time of day." I turned my back to her and opened my jeans drawer. "And it's not exactly that Grandpa 'lets us.' It's hard work. Really hard work. We've already been working for three hours this morning."

She didn't say anything, but I felt her scowling, and a few seconds later the tangled ball of shoelaces went sailing past my left shoulder and thunked against the mirror above my dresser.

"Hey!" I whirled around. "Why don't you just go back to sleep, Sara. Good grief, I can't believe what a grouch you are when you don't get your sleep out."

Tears sprang into her eyes. "I didn't want to come here in the first place!" She began banging her fists against her knees to emphasize each syllable. "I—DI—DN'T—WANT—TO—COME!"

"Shhh!" I hurried over and sat on the edge of her bed. "Sara, stop! Gram will hear you!"

She put her hands over her eyes, rubbing hard. "Today is the day the pool opens at home," she whimpered in a tiny, heartbroken voice, then listed over onto her side and pulled the covers over her

94

head. "My friends will go together and have, like, a huge party all day."

The snuffling sounds coming from her covers were so pathetic that I tickled where I thought her neck might be. "Hey, you can come out with us to do chores if you want. You can start tomorrow, okay?"

I really thought that since I'd called her bluff she'd say no thanks and go on snuffling, but she eagerly threw the covers off. "You mean it? Great! What should I wear and stuff? How do you think I should do my hair, braided? Or down, or pulled back with barrettes? And I have to think of what to wear. Get me up the second you get up, okay?"

"Okay," I said. "But you don't get dressed or fixed up for work like this. You just pull your hair back out of the way, cover it with a hat or scarf, and throw on one of the coveralls on the back porch. And—this is important, Sara—you wear a pair of those high-topped rubber boots that are lined up by the back door."

I stood and walked back to my dresser. I knew I should have felt happy about cheering Sara up, but something about her silly "what should I wear" questions made me feel really irritated.

The next morning I woke as usual at 4:15 and tried to wake Sara. But I couldn't. Surprise, surprise.

I shook her really hard, but she just kept elbowing me away.

"Leave me alone!" she finally growled in her sleep, and slapped at me wildly with both hands.

"Okay, but don't say I didn't try," I whispered to her, and went on out with a certain sense of relief.

Then at about 6:30, when Elijah and I were cleaning the stalls after the last of the cows had gone through, we heard the sucking sound of someone making their way toward us through the muck of the barnyard. Then the footsteps stopped, and seconds later Sara moaned.

"Ohhhh, you guys? Help, okay? Yuck!"

Elijah and I hurried to the door. Sara was standing birdlike on one foot about twenty feet from us. The foot folded up under her was covered only with a mud-splattered white sock. The red tennis shoe she balanced on was covered with mud so thick her foot looked like a chocolate-covered cherry. The other shoe, the one buried in ooze, wasn't visible at all except as a fast-disappearing footprint in the slime.

Elijah waded out to her. "Put your arms around my neck," he commanded quickly, and then carried her piggyback into the barn.

I slogged out too and dug into the muck for her lost shoe.

"Sara, didn't you hear me yesterday morning?" I scolded as I stomped back into the barn and threw the mud-ball of a shoe in the hay by the water faucet.

Sara was sitting barefoot on a hay bale, carefully wiping her hands with a rag Elijah had given her. "Sorry," she said, looking at me and then Elijah from under lowered lashes. "Dumb me, huh?" She smiled, hard, so the dimple in her left cheek deepened, and Elijah smiled good-naturedly back.

"I said to positively wear boots! Boots and a coverall, Sara! And those white jeans are positively the worst thing you could have worn. If you're out here for fifteen minutes they'll be ruined."

"Quit griping! I said I was sorry, okay?"

"What's going on?" Rennie had been cleaning some of the milking tubes in the back room of the barn. He frowned at Sara as he walked up to us. "What's she doing out here?"

Elijah shot Rennie a "let's be nice" look, but to tell the truth, I myself wasn't much in the mood to worry about how Rennie's blunt comment might hurt Sara's feelings.

"She came to help," I said dully, bending to gather up Sara's shoes and socks and throwing them in a feed bucket. I put the bucket under the water faucet, turned on the spigot, and crouched to begin scrubbing the hopeless-looking shoes.

"Oh, yeah, she'll be a huge help," Rennie said, then laughed his trademark sarcastic laugh. He walked over to me and turned off the water, jerked the half-filled bucket from under my hands, and swung it over toward Sara, sloshing a little water on her jeans in the process. "Clean up your own mess," he said to her.

"Rennie, she's barefoot and upset and wet," I began. "I can . . ."

"No!" he exploded. I heard the barnswallows in my hayloft laboratory above our heads leaving their nests in a frightened flurry.

Rennie had frightened Sara, too—right out of the tears it looked like she might have been about to shed. She looked from him to Elijah to me quickly, then stood, shook her head, and bolted, running barefoot and sliding through the mud, back to the house.

Rennie shook his head in total disgust.

"She was just trying to help us," I repeated quietly to him as I crouched back down by the bucket.

"Oh, right, Tory," he shot back. "Get real. She didn't even hang around to clean up her mess. Why should she? People like *her* always have people like *you* for that."

Still shaking his head, he went stomping away to finish his job in the back of the barn.

I looked up at Elijah and he shrugged and frowned. He seemed just as puzzled as I was at the intensity of Rennie's sudden rage.

Chapter 13

But even though I didn't understand why Rennie had gotten so furious, still his words got more and more under my skin. Why *did* Sara expect to be able to run away like that, to leave me with her dirty work? That afternoon I cornered her at the fishpond.

"Sara, I want to ask you something and I need an honest answer. Why did you ignore my advice about the boots? Why did you get all dressed up like that to come to the barn?"

She just lay there on her stomach like she hadn't heard, trailing one hand through the water and humming a little.

"Sara, answer me! Did you not hear me, or maybe not understand me when I said not to dress up to come out to the milk barn, and that boots were important?"

"Yes. No. Oh, I don't know. Victoria, why are you bugging me about it? I don't want to go out there with you guys again, anyway. Boy, you call me morning grouchy, but you guys are the ones. Grouchy, grouchy. Unbelievable.''

I yanked a clump of dandelions from their stems. ''I'm 'bugging' you because you caused us a lot of extra work this morning. I tried to explain to you that chores are hard, and we were definitely too busy to have to clean up after you.''

My heart was racing and I told myself to calm down, calm down. I really wanted Sara to understand, and getting upset wasn't going to help. ''Listen, here's the thing. Chores are a special time for us. It's like . . . okay, it's like cheering, Sara. You know how you and the other cheerleaders all work together, sort of like a machine? You don't have to show off or . . . or stand out. In fact, if somebody tries to do that they hurt the other people's feelings and kind of ruin things.''

''In cheering, each of us wants to do the best jumps and have the most spirit,'' she said, bouncing to her feet and doing a cartwheel that ended in a jump. ''I want to be the star. I want to look and perform the best because I want to be captain by next year. We all do. Give me a D! Give me an O! Give me a D! O! Do!''

I suddenly didn't want to be her audience, so I looked away, back to the fish. They were shifting through the clear water in a constantly changing pattern of orange and black.

''Well, then, Sara, you're probably right,'' I said, still without looking at her. I got to my feet and tossed my dandelions into the pond. ''What I'm talking about isn't like cheerleading at all.''

*   *   *

Sara, true to her word, never ventured into the cow barn with us again. When I came back to the house to change clothes after chores each morning I could count on finding her heavily asleep in almost the exact position she'd been in when I'd left our room three or four hours before.

She didn't complain again to me about being away from her friends in Milwaukee, either. Maybe she just accepted the situation, but I think it's more likely that after our conversations that day in the barn and later at the fishpond she decided I wasn't a very good audience for her complaints. We'd hardly ever argued before, and our argument that day blew over quickly, but the things that had come into the open to cause it still hung, invisible but important as air, between us.

Besides, back in Milwaukee I'd had lots of time for patiently listening to her chatter about her many thrills and her occasional problems. But here, I had my own busy life, and time was much more precious to me. As the summer routine sank into place, each long day seemed carved from the sweet golden light, and I hated to waste a single minute.

I awoke before dawn each morning itching to jump from bed and get started. Work in the barn became smoother and smoother, because though Rennie still occasionally pushed the limits and Elijah complained softly when he did, they were finally really getting along together. Grandpa called it "working in harness."

After the hard but satisfying teamwork of chores I

could look forward to rambling through the fields and puttering in my lab.

But best of all, by the third week of June, the haying and planting were winding down and Elijah was no longer working such long hours in the fields. Sort of as an extension of our "Rise and Shine Club," Elijah and Rennie and I began spending much of our time together. The three of us could be found most afternoons stuffing our faces with newly ripened apricots or wild blackberries, fishing at the pond beyond the machinery shed, or just sitting and reading or talking in the shade of the huge oak trees in the back yard.

Two or three times we wandered down to the old house, checked out the grounds, and made sure all the doors were locked. But we didn't see the boy all that month, hadn't seen him since Memorial Day, and in the bright June heat it became easier and easier to imagine he'd been just what Wade said he was—only a mirage.

I began to think of the tension between us all at the beginning of the summer as a distant and fading mirage, too. I suppose I thought if any trouble came, it would come from Sara, because she felt left out as the other three of us went our way.

But on the first day of July, Rennie unexpectedly pushed easygoing Elijah a step too far, and things between us took a sudden nosedive.

Chapter 14

That day dawned hot. As we followed Grandpa outside I noticed that my rubber boots were staying dry, even as I walked through the tall meadow grass. It hadn't cooled down below the dew point in the night, for the first time all summer.

Past the goldfish pond, Grandpa raised his left arm to tell us good-bye. He cut right to go to the machine shed through the murky light, while Elijah, Rennie, and I continued on toward the milking barn. The only sound was the distant howling of the coyotes, who always sounded like they knew they owned the dawn but had to stake a fresh claim each morning to be on the safe side.

Suddenly a new piece of farm equipment I hadn't seen before loomed in the thick shadows ahead. I'd often thought the farm machines, especially when cloaked by darkness or dawn shadows, looked like prehistoric beasts. The big silage cutter in particular, with its long elevated "neck," greatly resembled a brontosaurus or plesiosaur, and the tractors could have been shorter, squatter dinosaurs—triceratops, maybe, with their huge glass-encased cabs a little like bony hoods. The combine with its rotating reel could have been a stegosaurus with triangular plates running across its back.

As we drew a little closer I saw that this new machine was a huge metal wagon—really large, high-bellied, and thick-wheeled, with a long and elaborate tongue cocked up at an angle for fastening it to one of the bigger tractors. It seemed to me like a tyrannosaurus rex that first morning I saw it. Dangerous, hulking in wait, springing on us suddenly out of nowhere.

"What is that thing?" I asked Elijah. "Is it just a . . . a regular wagon? Why's it so big, and why does it go down to a point like that underneath?"

"It's the big gravity flow wagon," Elijah said. "Grandpa's had it at the elevator in Mulberry Grove for a while, but Wade brought it down last night to get a load of soybeans out of one of our bins. That thing you call a point is really a funnel. When Wade turns a wheel right above it, a door opens in a chute below that funnel and all the grain slides out in an avalanche. It makes emptying the wagon a million times easier than shoveling stuff out of a regular flat-bottomed wagon."

"Fantastic!" Rennie dropped the buckets he'd been carrying, and ran the last few yards to the wagon. When he was right beside it, I saw that it was nearly twice as high as he was tall. The top of the tires came nearly to his shoulders.

He was obviously looking for a way to climb onto the thing. In seconds he found it. There was a metal ladder attached to the back (the tail of tyrannosaurus), painted the same green as the rest of the wagon's body.

"Ya-hoo!" he called. "Watch this!"

He disappeared from our sight and then in seconds was standing on top of one of the wagon's high-walled sides. Arms out for balance, he began quickly walking that rim, about ten feet from the ground, around one corner, then around another, then another. Rennie Rimwalker. I don't know if that name occurred to me then, or before, when he'd walked the rims of the feed stall fences, or the attic beam of the old house.

Rennie Rimwalker, Captain Rennie Rimwalker. On top of the world, impressive and scary, irritating and breathtaking. Cherrysmatic. Grandpa would have a cow if he was out here with us right now and saw . . .

"Get down." Elijah's jaw was set, his face grim.

Rennie stopped, balancing nonchalantly, showing off, with his hands in the pockets of his cut-off shorts. Still, the same new dangerous edge I'd heard in Elijah's voice had obviously gotten through to him too, because he hesitated another full minute or so before shaking his head, laughing under his breath, and resuming his balancing act, walking faster this time. He was soon practically sprinting around the edge of

105

the wagon, loping along that narrow rim in dizzying circles.

"I said get down, Rennie. Now!"

Elijah's actions seldom surprised me, but I remember how surprised I was by the suddenness and intensity of his anger that morning.

"Hey, get a grip, Elijah." Rennie'd hit a smooth rhythm with his running—five strides along each of the long sides, two along the short ones. His words came out in little puffs as he ran. "Don't be such a boring old nag all the time, farmboy! Just do me a huge favor and lighten up."

Rennie must have been shaken up by Elijah's anger—he hadn't used that openly insulting tone with him since Memorial Day.

Elijah stepped forward, stood just below the wagon. "No, you do me a favor and quit showing off. It may impress your gang in San Diego, but out here it looks just plain stupid!"

I didn't realize I'd been holding my breath until all of a sudden my lungs ached. The sun was edging up, and the fields were hot pink and steamy. I'd never seen Elijah like this, so close to being out of control. Rennie stopped running and glared down at him, his eyes too bright, his sarcastic smile too forced-looking this time. There were two bright red splotches along the sides of his thick neck.

I made a weak attempt to joke them out of their standoff.

"You guys, the cows are calling us." But they

didn't seem to hear, or just ignored me like they were ignoring the increasingly loud, mournful mooing of the cows. And suddenly it was Elijah's turn to be openly insulting.

"It was bad enough when you took a chance on bringing the old house down around our heads by messing around on that rotten ceiling beam." Elijah's voice had a quiver to it. "And it's bad enough that you show off on that fence through the chores and keep the animals stirred up and nervous. But nobody goes clowning around on a machine like a gravity flow wagon. Not when I'm around to stop them, understand?"

"Oh, right, I'm just so sure that . . ."

Elijah kicked one wheel of the wagon, cutting Rennie off. "Answer me!" he yelled. "Do you understand, or not?"

Rennie stood staring for a second, then sat down on the rim, slid to one wheel, and jumped to the ground, inches from Elijah. He folded his arms across his chest and shook his head.

"I think you've lost it, Eli," he whispered, trying to use his trademark sarcasm, though he couldn't find the "cool" smile to go with it. "I've seen it all before, guys so insecure they can't stand the sight of anybody in control."

I'm not sure who pushed who first, and I don't know if either of them knew either. But all of a sudden Rennie was on the ground and Elijah was sprawled against the wheel of the wagon. Then they were on their feet, lunging toward each other, meeting and tangling together, falling, rolling on the ground, punching and kicking.

It had all come on so suddenly that it took me a while to get my wits and voice together.

"Stop it!"

To my great surprise, at the sound of my voice they stopped, and just sat there in the dirt as though they couldn't figure out exactly how they'd gotten there.

Elijah's lip was bleeding. He got to his feet, turned his back on Rennie, and went over to the buckets Rennie had dropped, picking them up with a jerk. Not looking in our direction, he walked on toward the milking barn.

"That's right, cousin," Rennie called to him. "Just ignore me like you ignore your own shortcomings. Put down in other guys what you're too chicken to copy, right? My father taught me to walk along mountain ridges without fear! He taught me to be a man, to be in control at all times."

Through a haze of misery, I glanced over at Rennie and got the biggest shock of the shocking morning.

"He taught me," Rennie said very quietly, and I could have sworn there were tears in his eyes.

Not knowing what to do, I mumbled to Rennie that I'd better help with the cows, and ran to the milking barn.

Elijah was setting up the milking paraphernalia, moving quickly, yanking things, breathing too fast.

"Elijah?" I whispered.

"People suffocate!" He was pale, as shaken up as Rennie had been. "Kids die every year from farm accidents—crushed under tractors, suffocated in gravity flow wagons. Can't he understand that? Does he think I like always having to be careful, careful, careful, always having to think and overthink like I'm an old man?" He ran both hands through his long hair, then turned around and hit both fists against the rough oak of the wall. "Sure I'd like to loosen up, to be more like Rennie, to just forget about risks and consequences. But everybody depends on everybody on a farm! One slip and other people get . . . get hurt."

He sat down hard on the concrete floor and put his head in his hands. I finished connecting up the tubes of the milking machines, then I went and sat quietly beside him, figuring he'd talk when he was ready.

Finally, he took a deep breath, let it out, and spoke quietly, like the words were being pulled from him.

"Back in Missouri, on the farm a mile down the road from ours, there were two little boys—Sam and Charlie Wilkins. They both got new coats for Christmas two years ago, and they fought over who got the shiny jacket, the blue baseball jacket—Kansas City Royals. Sam, the younger one, ended up getting it. He was only six, and Charlie was eight. Charlie ended up with the red corduroy coat. His mother sewed a St. Louis Cardinals patch on it, but she told my mother that Charlie was still disappointed—it just wasn't shiny, like a real baseball jacket."

Elijah snatched up a handful of hay, and let it go, picked it up again, and let it go. His hand was shaking.

"My dad and I were at the elevator a few weeks later when Charlie and Sam came with their father and uncle to unload some beans, from a gravity flow wagon. I was in the business office, drinking a Coke from the machine there. I didn't know what had happened till I heard the commotion, the voices, the yelling and running. I ran too, toward where trucks and wagons were lined up waiting to unload. There was a crowd around the Wilkins' wagon, where it was parked over the grate of the elevator pit, and there were some feed sacks on the ground. I saw little Charlie lying there, on those sacks, coughing and crying while some people gave him water, comforted him. Sam . . . Sam was nowhere I could see. It turned out he was . . . still in the beans, trapped under the beans."

I tried to say something, but my voice wouldn't work. Elijah looked from his hand, from his fistful of hay, up to me.

"When the chute of a gravity flow wagon is opened, the grain moves down like a whirlpool, or like quicksand," he said quickly, in almost a whisper. "It pulls down everything, anything that falls into it. Besides being suffocated, anything sucked beneath is crushed under three or even four tons of grain! Both Charlie and Sam fell in that day—they'd been horsing around, leaning too far over the edge, and in the blink of an eye they just sort of tumbled. Mr. Wilkins climbed up the wagon in time to grab for them, and he got Charlie. But . . ." Elijah stopped and swallowed. "But he said he just couldn't get a good enough hold on Sam's jacket. He felt his fingers slip across it, but then Sam was pulled under. Sam was just gone."

Elijah put his head in his hands again.

"Sam was only six years old, and his Royals jacket was just too slippery, just too slick."

"Oh, Elijah," I whispered. Suddenly the barn seemed too hot, too close, and I got up and made my way to the door, leaned against the rough wooden frame. I gulped down air, my eyes stinging. My heart felt like it was the thing being crushed in a golden sea of moving grain.

The sun was up and heat shimmered in dizzy waves above the fields. The clover was blooming, purple as deep shadows, and Moccasin Creek gleamed like a razor blade.

"Elijah!" I whirled around, but he was standing just a few feet behind me, looking out the doorway, over my shoulder, with his mouth slightly open.

"I see it," he whispered. "I see him."

The boy was back in the round window of the old house.

Chapter 15

Sara saw the boy too that morning.

In fact, Sara also saw everything that happened at the gravity flow wagon—Rennie's rimwalking, then the fight, Elijah and me going to the barn, and Rennie running in the opposite direction, down the road toward Mulberry Grove. Sara woke up early, probably because of the heat, and saw the fight out our west bedroom window, and then the boy out the east one.

"He's very lonely now," she said, sitting propped against her pillows while I dressed after my shower. She kept running her fingers through her Raggedy Ann's yarn hair, untangling it so she could braid it like she'd braided it so often when she was little.

"Who, Rennie?" I asked, yanking shorts from the second drawer of our shared dresser.

"No, the boy. He gets lonelier and lonelier. It's hard for him to watch you and Rennie and Elijah being together, having fun and stuff. It makes him feel left out, and sad. Very, very sad."

"How . . . how do you know that, Sara?"

"I just do."

"But nobody's even seen the boy since Memorial Day."

"I have," she said lightly. "I see him nearly e-ver-y, sme-ver-y single-mingle day."

Shock raced through my veins for a second, but then I noticed she was talking in a high, thin voice, a voice almost like a small child's. She had had an imaginary friend for a while when she was four or five and I had first left her to go to school. Maybe she was doing that again now, using the boy as an imaginary playmate, and only pretending she could see him so often.

I was glad that my back was to her. I couldn't stand to see the expression on her face. I kept thinking of Elijah's story, of Charlie losing his little brother, Sam. Sara wasn't used to doing things alone. She was becoming less herself, less Sara-like. Guilt made my hands fumble so that I took a long time buttoning my shirt. Then I went to sit beside her on her bed.

"Sara, listen, let's do something today. Just me and you."

She looked up from her braiding, her eyes bright as if a light had been switched on inside her head, her smile wide and happy. "You mean it? Don't you want to do stuff with the boys?"

I shook my head, still not quite able to meet her eyes.

"I just want to be with you, just us girls. You pick what you want to do and we'll do it."

"Well, let's see, we could blow bubbles with the

petunias like Gram taught me, and we could practice for a fish funeral, just in case,'' she chattered, planning. ''Then maybe decorate some matchbox coffins—I've only got six done, and there could be as many as a dozen deaths, if the whole pond should get poisoned or something.'' She was wriggling off the bed now, bouncing on her toes as she grabbed clothes from the dresser, excited, her old self. ''And then we can take lunch to Mr. Effingham! And I can tell you all about him on the way.''

Mr. Effingham, like the petunia bubble-blowing, was an idea of Gram's to keep Sara from feeling too bored. Mr. Effingham was a very old man who lived about a mile down the gravel road. He hadn't been feeling well, so Gram and Sara had been taking lunch to him every day for the past couple of weeks.

''Just don't—I repeat, DON'T—bite into that awful candy he gives you,'' she warned as she flew around the room, pulling on clothes.

Knowing she would inform me in detail later about that candy and everything else, I just played along.

''Okay, I won't,'' I said.

''On the other hand, whatever you do don't spit it out in front of him, and don't just put it in your pocket or he'll just give you another piece.''

''Okay, I won't.''

We waded through the fuzzy-stalked petunias that grew all over the side yard, picking the sturdiest and most open-looking to blow bubbles with. Then Sara

instructed me in the fine art of bubble soap-making—
half a bowl of water, and two tiny squirts of Palmolive
dishwashing detergent.

We sat for maybe an hour between two of the pillars
on the broad front porch, a pile of pink petunia
blooms like a soft fire between us, while Sara blew
soap bubbles and I looked frequently toward the old
house, shielding my eyes with my hand from the
bright sun. The boy wasn't there any longer, but my
nerves felt raw with the feeling that he would be back.
And what about Rennie and Elijah? Was the awful
fight this morning the beginning of the end of things
between them, and among the three of us? Had this
summer started out just too good to last?

"You blow, too," Sara suddenly ordered, and I got
busy and blew through the trumpet of a bloom,
watched bubbles form and cluster, then watched them
pop and drip onto my shorts.

"Pretty, huh?"

"Yeah, pretty," I answered.

Had Sara's activities always been this . . . pointless?

"By the way, Sara, I've been meaning to ask. How's
the trombone coming? Still think you'll make marching band this fall?"

She shrugged, filling her cheeks with air, blowing
into a soggy bloom.

"I haven't been hearing you, but I guess that's because I'm way up in the hayloft working in my field
lab most of the afternoon. Is that when you're practicing? Afternoons?"

"Maybe," she said, then slid from the porch, wiping her soapy hands on her legs. "Okay, now let's go check the fish!"

All twelve of the fish were alive, to Sara's thinly concealed disappointment. We spent a while on the kitchen porch with bits of ribbon and glue and Gram's stash of old matchboxes, making tiny, elaborate coffins. Meanwhile, Gram puttered in the kitchen, fixing the lunch we would take to Mr. Effingham.

"Whew! I'd just as soon not brave this heat myself," she said, coming out the screen door to hand us a basket, then fanning herself with the bottom of her apron. "You girls can manage to get this to Mr. Effingham without me, I'm sure."

Sara jumped to her feet. "Race you!" she called over her shoulder as she headed up the driveway.

"Nice to see my Sara so perky," Gram said, obviously to me. "I've worried about her here lately. Seems so left out, with you others always going your own way."

I got her point and felt guilty. "She's the one who goes her own way in Milwaukee. She's got about a zillion friends, and Mom ends up being her personal chauffeur all the time."

Gram didn't answer, and I knew that she considered my attitude strange and selfish. My words had sounded that way to my own ears, but still they'd been true, and I didn't want to take them back. Flustered, I ran off the porch to catch up with Sara.

* * *

She chattered about Mr. Effingham all the way to his house.

"His right thumb is missing! He cut his hand when he was a young man, and his jaws were locking up with tetanus, and they just cut it off—just like that! What do you think they did with it in the hospital? Buried it? Used something like a matchbox?"

"I doubt it. They probably just sort of, well, threw it away. I think that's what they do."

At the far edge of our property, three of Gram's brown hens pecked among the wilted vines of the strawberry patch. Sara knelt to grab one, and petted its slick feathers while it stood frozen, gurgling in its throat, obviously wondering uneasily what would happen next.

"Really? They throw pieces of you away?" She let go of the hen and grimaced. "Yuck!"

I smiled, remembering in a rush why everyone loved and coddled Sara at home. Sara was so much . . . here. Everything that happened to her seemed to be happening for the first time in the history of the world. Every thought she had seemed to be the first thought in anybody's head on that subject.

"Why shouldn't I bite into the candy?" I asked.

"Oh!" She gave three quick hops. "Mr. Effingham has this awful candy, these jellied orange slices. He just loves them, and he keeps them in a white paper sack in a bookcase in his living room. That's all there is in his living room—an old dusty bookcase and a kerosene heater and a couch with stuffing sticking out. In the kitchen all he's got is a big black stove and a round table and two chairs. I guess he's got a bed and stuff in his bedroom, but I've only been in the kitchen and living room. His whole house smells like kerosene because he heats with it. And bacon grease. He doesn't heat with bacon grease, but his house smells like it. And when you walk through, everything seems to shake, the walls and floors and stuff, and echo because it's so empty and everything. And dusty. I mean, it doesn't echo because it's dusty, it just IS dusty. And empty, empty, empty. Gram says it's only been empty like that since his wife died twenty years ago. They had a sale of all his furniture. There isn't anybody around here that belongs to him, that owns him.''

''What about the candy?'' I interjected quickly when she paused for breath.

''Oh! It breaks your jaw to chew it. It tangles up in your teeth. And besides, it tastes like the house smells, like bacon grease and kerosene. Once there were tiny ants on my piece. Gram saw them too and said, 'Honey, save your candy for later so's you don't spoil your supper, why don't you?' But Mr. Effingham said, really quick, 'Oh, it won't bother a meal, just that one little piece!' So I had to eat it, right then and there. I blew the ants off real quick, though, before I stuck it in my mouth.''

By this time we were turning onto the small footpath that led off the gravel road and down a hill to Mr.

Effingham's. I could see his bright green roof, and then gradually more and more of the small white house as we went down the steep hill. Someone had nailed chicken wire fencing from the roof of the porch to the floor, and there were huge purple flowers climbing up it, then rambling all over the eaves and drainpipe.

I saw the flowers long before I saw Mr. Effingham, though I guess he'd been standing there under them, waiting for us, all along. A tiny bent figure in faded blue overalls with wisps of white hair, he was as nearly invisible as the flowers were flamboyant.

Chapter 16

"**H**e keeps his teeth in a glass on the sink."

Sara whispered this one last tidbit breathlessly, then went skipping ahead, to where Mr. Effingham was standing perfectly still, but now with a wide single line of a smile drawn like a small child would draw it across his face. He had the gentlest eyes I'd ever seen, as though he'd seen everything sad and everything happy in his long life and it had left his eyes the lightest, most innocent of blues and his mind washed of all harmful thoughts. Everything about him was white or light blue, except for a red bandanna handkerchief pouring like his heart's blood from the left pocket of his faded chambray shirt.

"Well, there, girlie, girlie!" he crooned softly when Sara ran up and threw her arms around his waist. Sara was small, but Mr. Effingham seemed so fragile, like a stem of wheat. I was afraid she'd knock him over.

"This is my big sister, Victoria. She's fourteen and she's the smart one and likes bugs and rocks."

"Pleased to make your acquaintance," Mr. Effingham said, slowly extending his right hand. I shook it, trying hard not to stare at the hole where his thumb had been. His skin felt cool, papery.

"Your house is very pretty, hidden away like this," I said, looking into his amazing eyes. "Your flowers are just gorgeous."

"Clematis." He moved his head, turned it slowly upward and around like a turtle, following the purple cloud of flowers. "Anna planted them some, oh, must be fifty years ago. Could be sixty. They just go on year after year. Things just go on."

The locusts suddenly began humming louder, so loud it set my ears ringing.

"The insects are saying it would be a good fishing day," Mr. Effingham said. His voice was slow, so gentle and quiet I could hardly hear him over the locusts. "If'n I wasn't feeling so poorly, we'd roll us some potato pieces in flour and bacon grease, and give the fish at the branch creek a run for their money."

"Do they bite on that?" I asked.

He smiled his pencil-line smile again, and narrowed his eyes as though thinking. "Well, I don't rightly know. They never have, but then they've never bit on worms when I've fished either."

"Gram made you chicken," Sara said, bouncing on her heels, impatient with our conversation. "Here."

She held out the basket, and he took it in both

hands and bent slowly to put it gently on the porch floor.

And then, his remarkable eyes lit up a little. I thought of how the last rays of sun throw a quick brightness over the sky at twilight.

"Time for a treat, girlies," he said, clapping his hands once in a slow-motion way. He slowly turned and even more slowly opened his screen door. A strong whiff of bacon grease came from the kitchen. "Care to come inside, or will you wait here?"

"We'd better wait here," I answered, though I could feel Sara contrarily putting her hands on her hips. I could see how tired he was, and didn't think we should bother him much longer.

When he'd completely disappeared into the shadows of his kitchen, Sara rolled her eyes at me. "Here it comes. Brace yourself, it's toothache time."

I put my finger to my lips, smiling at her around it, and we stood there under the purple clematis canopy with the locusts droning piercingly for what seemed like an hour, until Mr. Effingham reappeared, holding a wrinkled white sack carefully in both hands like a treasure.

"Here, now, ye each have you a piece," he whispered, coming out through the screen, letting it slam behind him.

"Oh, now, we don't want to eat up all your candy!" I protested.

But he slowly unrolled the paper and held the open sack out to us in his thumbless hand.

"Now, don't you worry about that," he said, chuckling soundlessly. His eyes gleamed, sending that gentleness out toward us in waves. "I'll tell you what, you each take you two if you want to! One for now, one for later, heh?"

I licked my lips, and reached in the sack. "Thank you, Mr. Effingham."

Sara followed. "Thank you, Mr. Effingham."

We stood there gingerly holding our sticky jellied orange slices, smiling broadly and uneasily.

"Well, go ahead. Go ahead! You don't have to wait, just eat up!" Mr. Effingham seemed positively ecstatic.

We looked at each other, and popped our candy in our mouths, still grinning around it. Instantly I tasted kcrosene and bacon grease and felt my teeth cementing together.

Mumbling and gulping around the juicy candy, we said good-bye to Mr. Effingham, who stood there nodding and waving back at us.

When we got back to the house, Gram was working in the rocking chair on the kitchen porch. She was halving apricots, getting ready to make jam. "How was Mr. Effingham today?"

Sara sat down at her feet and began to chatter, settling in to give her the long version of our morning's activities. I took the opportunity to slip away, out to my sanctuary, my hayloft lab.

I needed to be alone, to think, to try and figure out

what was going to happen next between Rennie and Elijah, and between Sara and me. Would Rennie and Elijah make up? Could I get Rennie to accept Sara better? Did I, well, really want him to?

That thought made me shiver with self-disgust. Of course I wanted the boys to include Sara. Period. I told myself not to even think of such things. Think of something else.

Like the boy in the window. Just when we'd decided he was a reflection or a mirage, here he was back and then gone again. Gone for good this time?

I began climbing the rickety hayloft ladder and went from bright afternoon to shadows, from heat to cool, from farm sounds to quiet broken only by the grumbling of the barnswallows. I had the now-familiar sensation of shedding my skin, like a snake. Of lightening myself, making myself pure me.

The open loft window threw a square of house-shaped light on the oak floorboards. As though the light was pulling me, I left the ladder and walked over to stand in the middle of that little house design.

And right there and then, for the first time in my life, I really felt my body. I was suddenly aware of the muscles of my legs and back, newly strong from chores and hiking through the fields. I felt the taut ligaments and flexible bones holding everything so neatly and tightly together, the smooth and even work of my lungs as they breathed. That golden light caught and held me and excitement spread like electricity through my veins.

One of the tables Grandpa and I had made with plywood and sawhorses was filled with my collections, but the other was empty. I ran to the empty table, tipped the plywood up and let it slide to the floor, where it landed with a "whump" and whirled hayseeds through the air. Grunting, I pulled one long sawhorse across the floor and lined it up with the other one. Together they formed a perfect balance beam, not much more than an inch wide, maybe ten feet end to end.

I closed my eyes, took several deep breaths, then hoisted myself up and onto the end of that balance beam. I expected that I'd fall, only a three-foot drop to the floor. But though I expected it, I didn't expect it in the same way I'd always expected to fall from the balance beam at school, or to be chosen last for teams, or expected not to be able to do a chin-up, or expected not to run around the mile track without slowing to a walk. I'd expected those things to happen because I felt too weak and uncoordinated and gawky for them not to happen. Now I really didn't feel weak at all. I guessed that I'd fall. I was prepared to fall. But there was also a chance I would rimwalk instead. That's why my heart was beating so fast—there was a definite chance, I felt it.

I balanced for a few seconds on the end of the sawhorse, then extended my arms like a bird taking flight, and walked.

And I didn't fall, the whole length, so I turned and went back, faster, then back again, faster still. And then I was laughing as I practically ran from end to end of the beam, then stopped in the middle and balanced like a dancer on one foot.

I could do this! Cocky, I fell, got up and climbed on again, and ran from end to end. I jumped off, went over to where the roof slanted and was supported by a beam a couple of feet higher than my head. I jumped up to grasp the beam, and slowly, slowly chinned myself.

I dropped to the floor, rubbed my hands, and did it again—chinned myself! I'd never in my life been able to chin myself once, and now I'd done it twice.

"Yes, yes, yes!" I jumped around and did a little dance through the hay dust I was kicking up.

"Not bad," a voice said, as a shape emerged from the deep shadows in the corner. "Really, Tory, not too shabby. I'm impressed."

Chapter 17

"**R**ennie!"

A swirl of feelings hit me, as they always did when I found myself alone with Rennie. I was tongue-tied, angry, and fascinated all at once. That awful embarrassed grin spread across my face and I turned my back to hide it.

"Sorry about sneaking up on you," he said.

"That's okay," I mumbled. But then, I forced myself to turn and face him. "No, Rennie, it's really not okay. This is my place. Mine."

To my surprise, my idiot grin dissolved, and my face felt like my face again. "I mean, you could call to me before you come up, and use the ladder instead of your rope," I finished, more softly.

He shrugged. "No problem," he said, and sauntered over to my collecting table. "In fact, it's about time you got the guts to stake your claim to what's yours."

He was praising me for being selfish, like him. I

knew it wasn't right for his compliment to make me feel good, but still, it did.

"All these little boxes," Rennie said. "All these little sets." He picked up a moth that was lying by itself on the table, and held him toward me, frowning.

"It wouldn't fit," I answered his unspoken question. "My moth boxes are all full, and that one's plain, ordinary."

"So that makes him disposable," Rennie mumbled, dropping the moth on the table. "Somebody's always just outside. Have you noticed that?"

He moved to my makeshift balance beam, pounced up onto it gracefully as a tiger would, and did a handstand.

"Boy, Elijah is just so far off base sometimes it's truly pathetic," he called over to me, his voice husky with exertion as he balanced upside down.

I braced myself, sure he was about to launch into a sarcastic put-down of Elijah's "old man" cautiousness, his "farmboy" attitudes. Would I have the nerve to try and explain and defend Elijah to him?

Rennie's arms shook with the strain as he bent his elbows and slowly lowered his body to stretch his legs out parallel with the floor. He seemed to totally defy gravity for a few seconds, then he shoved off with his arms and landed in a crouch.

He straightened up and began clenching his hands to flex his fingers.

"Like that crack he made this morning about me impressing this gang of people, this bunch of friends or something, back in San Diego."

I couldn't believe that was the part of this morning's awful argument Rennie remembered the best.

"Well, I guess Elijah is a little . . . a little jealous of you sometimes."

Rennie stared at me, and there was something almost eager, almost hungry in his eyes. "Why?"

I felt I'd gone too far. I knew Elijah would never have admitted to jealousy of Rennie's free-and-easy ways, though every day I saw envy in his eyes. Envy or something awfully close to it.

"Well, Elijah's probably sort of a loner at home," I tried, in my stumbling way, to explain. "He lives so far from town, and his family depends on him so he can't just, well, cut loose. And Rennie, I doubt if you can understand how it is to be . . . quiet, shy. How it is for people to just not really notice you, to not really . . . include you. I mean, you're so obviously outgoing, you don't know how it feels to be practically invisible."

He kept looking at his hands, even though he'd stopped flexing his fingers. "I suppose if you're invisible, at least you don't have to worry about being seen but just purposely ignored," he finally said quietly, then looked in my eyes. "I mean, what makes Elijah think I have this big gang back home, anyway?"

His honesty took me by surprise and left me off-balance. I don't know why Elijah, Sara, and I assumed that he was popular, but I know we all did. At least popular in the off-center way rebels and daredevils seem always to be popular.

"Aunt Crystal keeps telling my father that you have

lots of friends," I said, deciding against describing those friends.

Rennie snickered, and shook his head. "Yeah, that's what she thinks. When trouble happens in our neighborhood, she assumes I've been in on it, just because I'm not home much."

I was hoping he'd say more, but he was interrupted by a long grumble of thunder. The wind came up along with it, and the patch of window light on the floor dimmed and flickered as the sky became overcast.

Following the thunder was a second sound, hard to identify at first. It sounded like a wounded animal—I immediately thought of Bruno, Grandpa's big, bad-tempered bull. But then it more or less took the shape of a scale of notes, coming from the far side of the house.

"Sara's finally practicing," I said. "She must have set up her stand out in the apricot orchard."

Rennie laughed, scornfully. "I bet Sara has never in her life had to work hard for a single thing she's gotten," he said. "I can spot her type a mile away."

"Oh, she's always trying out for things," I automatically protested. "She's been in lots of clubs, and made cheerleader for next year. Everybody adores her."

"Exactly," Rennie said. "I'll bet because she's just so, so adorable she's gotten by on looks and charm all her life." He walked back over to my collecting table, picked up the box of blue and black Monarch butterflies. "I'll bet she's just like these, flitting around, never sticking with one thing longer than a butterfly sticks with a flower."

"Rennie, I really think you're too hard on her," I said quietly. "Sara's okay. She's a good kid. Really."

Rennie put the butterflies down and folded his arms across his chest.

"Face it, Tory," he said. "Your spoiled little sister is a butterfly, and this poor, rejected moth could be you. Or me or Elijah. No matter how hard we work at things we all three know how it feels to be an outsider, just past the cut-off point."

I tried to laugh at that, but my throat was suddenly tight.

"Just don't be afraid to claim what's yours and to leave behind what isn't," he said as he moved toward the ladder. "Whether she's a 'good kid' or not, you don't own responsibility for Sara being constantly happy."

He started down the ladder, but stopped and looked back up at me. "By the way, I've been meaning to ask. How does Sara spell her name? Without an 'h' on the end, I'll bet, right?"

"Right, but how'd you know?" I asked.

He shrugged, smiling mysteriously. "How'd I guess you were a Tory? Butterfly Saras just don't use an 'h,' that's all."

And then he disappeared down the ladder. And I was left thinking, searching my mind for a time when, really, Sara HAD worked hard for something.

Conversation definitely lagged at the dinner table that night. It was so hot, so humid. And the tension between Rennie and Elijah was like a living thing, an uninvited guest.

Sara tried talking about her trombones. But even she ran down quickly, as though she was breathless under the weight of the storm clouds gathered both inside and out.

Just before dessert, Gram looked out the south window, where the cornfields began.

"I always start to feel a little claustrophobic when the corn gets shoulder-high," she sighed. "Tillie Myerson doesn't allow corn planted anywhere between her house and any of the other houses in her part of Irishtown. She likes an unobstructed view of things going on around her, and the older I get, the more I do agree with her thinking."

"Best to use the land for better purpose than to spy on your neighbors as Tillie does," Grandpa grumbled mildly.

No one else said much of anything. It was just too hot to think or talk or move. And Elijah and Rennie seemed to silently smolder, making the room even hotter.

As I carried my dishes to the kitchen, I noticed the sun was growing more red and swollen as it approached the ground. The clouds above it were purplish-black as a bruise.

I ran water in the sink, added soap, and began

thrashing it around wildly and more wildly. I wasn't sure what was suddenly making me so crazy with frustration until Rennie and Elijah came into the kitchen a few minutes later. Elijah was purposely hanging back like he had at the beginning of the summer, keeping a few feet between them as they brought in the rest of the uneaten food, the dirty dishes. Rennie was acting nonchalant in a stiff, forced sort of way, obviously pretending Elijah was on the moon and not right behind him.

"Okay, I've had it," I said, slamming a pan into the drainer so hard a bunch of bubbles blew from the sink and onto the floor. Luther ran in from the dining room to lick at them.

"You guys follow me," I demanded.

"What?" Rennie protested. "Hey, we've got work here to . . ."

"Now!" I glared first at Rennie, then at Elijah, then whirled around and slammed out through the screen door.

I guess they were too shocked to disobey, because they followed me as I stomped around the porch, jumped off the side, and waded through the long grass into the apricot orchard. When I turned to face them, they were standing a few feet apart, meek and shame-faced as toddlers caught playing in the street.

"What is the matter with you two guys?" I grabbed my hair in both hands, then threw up my hands, exasperated. "Why are you acting like such . . . such total jerks?"

"What?" Rennie asked, his eyebrows up in an expression of complete, infuriating innocence. "Hey, I was just . . ."

"Be quiet, Rennie! I'm out of patience with you! I've seen your room, remember? That dumb act may work on other people, but I know you now, Rennie! I saw your books, I know you read, I know you think, so just act as smart as you are and quit putting Elijah down! That first day, Memorial Day, you told Elijah he wasn't your friend, and he is, Rennie! He is your friend, and you know he is, so quit saying things that hurt his feelings!"

Rennie stared at the apricot-seed-covered ground.

"And you, Elijah," I said, going to stand right in front of him with my hands on my hips. "You admire Rennie—why can't you admit that to yourself? You could learn something from the way he takes risks, Elijah. You and I both could, and you know it."

I'd had my say, my anger was gone, and I felt like a balloon with the air all released—flimsy and empty. To my horror, tears started leaking out of my eyes. I collapsed to the ground and sat cross-legged among the hard little apricot seeds, my face in my hands.

"I don't want this to happen!" I sobbed. "You said to start claiming things that are mine, Rennie, and more than anything I want to reclaim this summer. This was starting out to be the best summer of my life, because of you two. Because of us. Because I was getting strong, and maybe even starting to . . . to get less afraid."

The locusts were the only sound for a while, then—

"Starting to get unafraid?" Rennie mumbled. "Hey, anybody who can give a lip-lashing like that sounds like a rough, tough expert in fearlessness to me."

Then Elijah laughed, and I wiped my eyes on the back of my hands and looked up to see them each extending a hand down to pull me up.

"Hey, man," Rennie said to Elijah, and cleared his throat. "I'm, you know, sorry about this morning."

"Yeah, right, me too," Elijah answered quickly.

I felt nearly weak-kneed with relief for a few seconds, but then the darkness suddenly grew much deeper, and the wind came up stronger and tossed the little clover heads in front of us so they bowed on their stalks like servants.

Everything took on an eerie sheen, and I thought the full moon had risen, luminous, over the fields. But where was the moon?

"Look!" Elijah pointed toward the old house.

A very white face peered at us from the round attic window. It seemed to actually give out light.

"Do you believe in magic?" Rennie asked, his voice high and fast and excited in the darkness.

Chapter 18

We all laughed, uneasily, though, at Rennie's question.

"Americus," I heard myself whisper.

"What?" Both boys turned to me.

"He was . . . he was our great-great-uncle." The wind hissed through the clover blossoms, and I had the sensation of talking in a crowd of other whisperers, telling only one of many secrets being told that windy night. "Gram said he died when he was only a little boy, just as that house was being built. I think she sometimes sees the boy, like we do. And I also think she thinks it's . . . him. Americus."

"Oh, come on," Rennie snorted a laugh. "You mean she thinks it's a . . . you mean a . . ."

". . . ghost," Elijah finished for him in his flat, logical way. "Listen, maybe somebody is playing a trick on Gram or something, and maybe we can stop them. Our first step would probably be to learn more about this little kid ancestor of ours. This Americus."

"Good, where do we start?" I asked eagerly. "I don't think we should tell Gram what we're doing, do you?"

Elijah shook his head. "You saw how weirded out she got when you tried to talk to her about the boy on Memorial Day. We'll handle our research on our own."

"And SO we BEGIN . . ." Rennie said in a silly monster voice, wiggling his fingers spookily through the air, "at the good old family plot at the cemetery!"

"Good a place as any," Elijah agreed.

I lay in bed for a long time too keyed up to sleep that night. So many things had happened during the long day, and now there was a storm coming and the air felt electric with it. Finally, I tiptoed past Sara's bed, over to the east window, and knelt there, looking out into the dark, dark night.

I felt the oak boards beneath my knees, and thought of how old they were, over seventy-five years. Sara's and my great-grandfather and his brothers had cut them from trees on this land, had planed them and hammered them. But these boards were young, compared to those in the house across the clover field.

That house was invisible in the darkness now. The boy was gone from the window.

I thought of all the young girls who had slept in long, linen gowns in both the houses. I thought of all the dinners eaten, all the summertime lemonade drunk, all the soldiers sent to war.

I thought I could see McKendree Chapel Cemetery, and yet I wasn't sure. It was two miles away out there, and though my eyes were focused toward it, it was too dark to tell if the deeper darkness I was seeing was the cemetery hill or only—deeper darkness, gathered storm clouds.

The wind lifted the white gauze curtains like arms around me.

Thunder rumbled. How could Sara sleep so soundly through this wind? Her Raggedy Ann doll had slipped from her bed and was lying on the floor. I picked it up, looked at it, absentmindedly set it on the wide window ledge.

Then I crept back to my own bed, burrowed under the covers, and went to sleep just as the storm broke around us.

I woke a few hours later to find the rain blowing in the open east window. I stumbled out of bed to shut the window, and noticed pink fingers of light cutting through the gray clouds. It was time to get up for chores, then, although it seemed I'd hardly slept.

Sara's Raggedy Ann still leaned against the corner of the window casing. She looked different. I picked her up, and she was soggy, soaked clear through.

I touched her tangled hair, which Sara had never gotten around to braiding, and streaks of dye red as blood came off on my fingers. Something looked so strange about her that I carried her into the bathroom that adjoined our bedroom, closed the door so I wouldn't wake Sara, and switched on the light.

The doll had round eyes the size of quarters, made of bright turquoise felt and attached to black yarn eyelashes. Where the rain had hit her face, the color from her eyes had run in bright streams.

Sara's doll was crying, bright blue tears, clear down her body.

"Oh. Oh, no." I drew in my breath, and felt my throat tighten. Sara's favorite doll was ruined. It was my fault.

I held her to my chest as if she were a real girl I could comfort, as if her tears could be just dried away, as if she weren't hopelessly stained.

I looked up at my own reflection in the bathroom mirror.

My eyes looked stricken and sad, like they always looked when something was hurting Sara, when something made her stop laughing, stop being her normal bubbly self.

Then Rennie's voice drifted through my head— ". . . you don't own responsibility for Sara . . ."

At the thought of Rennie I remembered last night in the apricot orchard, how close the three of us had been. For a while I'd been so afraid our friendship had been doomed by the morning's events, but it ended up strengthened by them instead.

I squinted at myself in the mirror. "Sara's too old for dolls anyway," I thought, and my eyes took on a different, harder but freer expression.

During chores that rainy morning Elijah, Rennie, and I made plans to go look for Americus' grave in

McKendree Chapel Cemetery late that afternoon, when we could all three slip away for a couple of hours without arousing anyone's interest.

The rain and mud slowed down our work, made herding the cows and feeding the other livestock difficult. Since I hadn't slept much I was very tired when I came back to the house, and all I could think of was a shower and a nap.

Sara and Gram were in the kitchen. Gram was in her chair by the window, and Sara, still in her nightgown, was on the floor beside her, with her head in Gram's lap. The ruined doll was on the kitchen table, and Sara was crying softly, whimpering while Gram stroked her hair.

At the screech of the door, Gram looked quickly over at me.

"What's wrong?" I asked, letting my voice rise more than I wanted it to on the last of those two words. I knew I didn't sound sympathetic as much as I sounded . . . accused, caught in the act of something.

"Look, Victoria!" Sara said, jumping up to grab the doll by the hair and holding it up in front of me. "Look, she's . . . she's awful. We can't fix her. She's ugly and ruined!"

I took the doll, pointedly smoothing down the hair Sara had just pulled upright. "Poor Annie. But, Sara, don't you think you've outgrown dolls, really?"

Sara grabbed back her doll, then let out another long, shuddering sob. "But I loved her!"

The door opened again, and Rennie came in behind me.

"Look," Sara pleaded, holding the doll toward him, letting her chin quiver a little. Maybe she thought this tragedy would be the thing that would finally make him open up and be nice to her. Or maybe she just needed sympathy from many directions, as she always seemed to need every kind of available attention.

Rennie glanced quickly at the doll and turned away.

"Big deal," he muttered as he started upstairs.

"Oren!" Gram said, standing up, moving to put her hands protectively on Sara's shoulders.

"Well, sorry, but it's just a stupid toy," he mumbled, then turned around to look directly at me. "Right, Tory?"

I opened my mouth, but stood helplessly looking from Rennie to Sara to Gram, unable to say a word. Rennie shook his head, turned away, and walked on upstairs.

Sara watched him disappear, then her forehead crumpled and she began to sob harder. She threw the doll on the table, face down, and ran from the kitchen, back toward our room.

"Well?" Gram said, looking in my eyes, waiting for something from me.

Exhaustion moved into me in one hard wave, and anger brighter and sharper than I was used to feeling came with it.

"Gram, didn't you see her? Sara holds the doll by the hair, she throws her down on her face like that when she's through using her to get sympathy from everybody. Meanwhile everybody laps it all up and puts her on a pedestal! What about me, Rennie, Elijah? Look at me!"

I was in my muddy work coveralls and my clunky milking boots—soaked, my hair stringing. I held my arms out so she could, hopefully, compare the sight of me to the sight of Sara just now, still in her pristine nightgown, coddled.

"Honey, if the chores are becoming too much for you, just talk to Grandpa about it," Gram said softly, sympathetically. "There's no need to exhaust yourself out there in the barn."

Her sympathy made me feel confused and worse than ever. Without a word I turned and slammed back outside.

I ran away from the house and past the fish pond, then stopped as I saw the light in the barn go out. Seconds later, Elijah came through the rough barn door and began the long trudge to the house through the deepening mud. I ran toward him, and when he saw me, he stopped walking and waited, surprised.

"Elijah! Tell me the truth! Am I . . . am I supposed to be Sara Moore's big sister all my life? I mean, is that what I am? All I am?"

Rain was dripping from his nose and eyelashes, and he took one hand and ran it over his face, but didn't suggest that this conversation could wait for a different, drier time. In fact, he didn't even give me a fast answer, but stood for at least a full minute, thoughtfully staring down at the mud.

"Of course you're not just Sara's big sister," he

finally said slowly. "But if it feels that way, maybe it's been easier for you to admire her than to learn to admire yourself."

I tried for a joke, though my throat throbbed. "What's to admire about me? I'd gladly learn, but there's nothing to study."

He looked at me and didn't even smile. "See what I mean?"

Chapter 19

I slept deeply the rest of the rainy morning, and woke disoriented a little before noon. In the kitchen Gram and Sara were bustling around packing sandwiches into the big wicker picnic basket, and Elijah was filling the big thermoses with water and with lemonade.

"We're going to Cavendish Woods to pick hickory nuts!" Sara called over to me, where I stood groggily leaning against the doorjamb. "All of us! We're going in the hay wagon and taking a picnic."

I noted with begrudging admiration that she was completely recovered from her huge tragedy this morning. Sara was like the sun in July—no cloud seemed to block her rays for long.

"Grandpa and Wade say it's too muddy to work in the fields this afternoon, so this will give us all a nice little break," Gram explained, smiling toward me.

I glanced at Elijah, who looked over at me sideways from his place at the sink. He mouthed the word

144

"tomorrow," and I understood that our cemetery expedition was postponed.

"How do you pick hickory nuts?" I mumbled, grouchy, still trying to wake up. "The trees are too high."

"The nuts will have started to fall from the trees. You gather them from the ground," Gram said, and came to give me a quick hug. "Feel better now?"

"More rested," I replied, to keep the record straight. If she thought I wouldn't have complained about Sara unless I'd been sick, she was wrong, and something new and tough inside me wanted her to understand that.

Wade drove the small tractor, the ancient John Deere, and the rest of us piled into the old wooden hay wagon. Cavendish Woods was about eight miles from the farm, and edged up against the Kankakee River. The soil there was spongy and rich, but flooded far too often for people to farm it or build houses, so the land was uncleared and the woods were as they'd been hundreds of years before, dark and lush. That was the reason for the tractor and wagon—there weren't roads back to the stand of old hickory trees, just rutted wagon paths that wove past old caves and limestone outcroppings.

It was beautiful back there in the woods, with the sound of the rushing river in the near distance. Beautiful and forbidding, dark and wet and primeval-looking. I hoped I'd get a chance to search for insects

145

when we'd finished filling our ten-gallon buckets with hickory nuts. I could imagine beetles growing huge and shiny in that dense humidity.

The ruts in the path got deeper and muddier as we approached the river, and we all held onto the edges of the wagon and jerked and swayed as Wade negotiated slowly through the trees.

And then, far to our right, a bridge appeared—a fragile black spiderweb over the river.

"Wow," Rennie breathed, sounding completely awed.

"I didn't know there was a bridge here across the Kankakee," Elijah said. "I thought you had to drive to Mulberry Grove and cross on the big Interstate bridge there."

"That's the old Cavendish Crossing Bridge," Grandpa answered, pointing with his pipe stem. "When I was a boy there was plenty of traffic acrost it, mules and horses pulling wagons such as this one. It was never open to automobiles, though. Just not made to bear that kind of traffic and weight. And for, oh, thirty years it's been closed to any traffic at all. There's big holes rotted in the timbers now, and the whole thing could collapse of its weight any fine day."

I saw then that there was a chain sealing off the opening of the bridge, with a sign, probably warning people to keep away.

"Wow," Rennie said again, in a whisper this time.

"It's wonderful," I whispered, because it was. It

146

hung so delicately over the water that it seemed magical, like something from a fairy tale. I was used to bridges with lots of steel and concrete, not to bridges that seemed stitched to the clouds with black embroidery floss.

"It's the king of all rims, that's what it is," Rennie said.

Elijah and I both looked at him then, and I think we both saw the same thing in his eyes.

Because three hours later, when all the cans were full of nuts, when we had eaten our lunch from the picnic hamper, when Grandpa, his old straw hat pulled over his face, was snoring gently, and Luther was asleep with his head on Wade's chest, when Gram was leaning against a tree, pretending to read the newspaper she'd brought from home but actually beginning to doze, then Elijah stood up and whispered to Rennie and me, "Okay, let's go."

And we got up quickly, eager to slip into the woods before any of the grown-ups woke up and asked questions.

"Wait up!" Sara called.

We stopped, and I turned back toward her. "You're supposed to stay here," I called softly, putting a finger to my lips. "We'll be right back. Don't wake Gram!"

I didn't give her time to argue, just turned away like she didn't exist, hissed a "Hustle!" to the boys, and without looking back ran full-speed toward the deep green wall of trees that thickly lined the river.

* * *

As we got close to the bridge I could see that the cables were rusting, some hanging broken and loose, and huge holes gaped in the rotten wooden beams that wagons and horses had once wheeled and clopped slowly across.

The last few hundred yards to the entrance we waded through weeds above our waists, and there were surely water moccasins skimming through the swampy underbrush beneath our feet.

But I wasn't thinking about that. My heart was beating so hard it hurt, because someway I understood that we were all three going to walk this rim. Not the rotted-out floor of the bridge, but one of the two chest-high iron spans that ran its length.

Today was the day we would all become Rimwalkers, and this was the way we'd do it. It seemed that clear and that simple.

We stopped near the entrance, on a little patch of gravel a few yards from the thick chain with a rough wooden sign bearing the single word—BEWARE.

Rennie started to run forward, but Elijah grabbed his elbow.

"Me first," Elijah said quietly, and walked forward to stoop under the chain.

Holding a cable, he climbed mountaineer-like onto the span, then let go and went easily and gracefully across the length of the bridge, surefooted, cool, calm but careful. When he reached the far side, he was so far from us he looked like a black-haired doll. He jumped off, crossed over to climb onto the opposite span, and came back across. I wasn't at all surprised at how naturally he did it. I knew he did far harder, more tricky balancing acts all the time in the course of farm work, he just didn't do them purposely as stunts.

"All right." Rennie nodded admiringly.

"Now me," I heard myself say. "Before I chicken out."

"I'll walk along right beside you," Elijah said quickly. "If you start to fall, I'll grab you. If you feel too afraid, jump down onto the bridge, I'll be sure you don't fall through."

It seemed like too good an idea for me to argue with, so I didn't.

I really don't remember too much what it was like, walking that long span under the drizzly sky that day, the river churning so far below me, the wind light but gusty. I mostly remember I was scared to death, absolutely terrified. I could hardly breathe, but kept my legs moving, one in front of the other. I tried not to look down, toward the river, tried to keep in mind that that was Elijah's dark head below me on the bridge side, that I was safe.

But I wasn't perfectly safe, and I knew it. I could have fallen, and Elijah could have reached and grabbed a microsecond too late to stop me. Besides, I was walking between two things—the family I knew, and the wilderness at the far end of the bridge that I didn't know at all. And the thing connecting one to the other was narrow and slippery. If I got giddy, terrified with that thought, I'd lose my bearings, and my balance. I knew it.

Still, I walked the bridge span, across and back. It

took a long, long time. Near the end I was shuffling, like a small child taking its first steps along the edge of a sofa.

When I finally was finished, I let Elijah help me off the span. He held up the chain while I ducked unsteadily under, then I slid down into the grass and just sat there shaking while Rennie walked, danced, performed along the span like a circus acrobat.

Walking the rim of the old Cavendish Crossing Bridge that day was the stupidest and bravest thing I'd ever done.

The sun was low and the shadows were deep as we left Cavendish Woods. The storm clouds had finally drifted on east, and the intense heat of the day before was threatening to return.

It was strange to sit there so near the adults, knowing we'd just done something that would give them all heart attacks if they knew about it, but knowing that they'd never know about it, ever.

I remember feeling perfectly happy as we bumped along the rutted roads, out of the trees and into the twilight. It was the kind of intense happiness that I assumed would dull back to contentment soon, like Christmas morning happiness, or birthday party happiness.

But it didn't. That sharp pencil point of happiness continued to draw the shape of my days after that, for the rest of the weeks of hot July.

Chapter 20

A day or two after the picnic, one of Gram's goldfish died. Sara spent the entire afternoon and evening silently bustling around, preparing for the funeral she'd already spent most of June planning. When I came in from chores the next morning, there was a funeral invitation (written on a napkin) centered on my pillow, addressed to all three of us—Elijah, Rennie, and me.

I read the invitation three times, then stood remembering myself and the boys, running toward the bridge. I pictured Sara, small in the background, calling us—"Wait up!" I'd lied so easily and quickly. "You're supposed to stay here . . ."

I told the boys I thought we ought to attend Sara's fish funeral. "Give me a break!" Rennie howled, but I stared him down before he could rip into the laughter I knew was coming.

"Rennie, listen, don't you think we . . . owe her this?"

I knew "owe" wasn't the right word, but I couldn't put into words exactly what I DID mean.

"If she wants our company so bad she doesn't have to stage baby games like this to get it," he said. "She could join us in breathing the delicious morning aroma of the cow barn, right?"

"Right, I guess. But she's just not the . . . type for that."

"My point exactly," Rennie mumbled.

"Let's just go," Elijah said in the calm way that always seemed to decide things for us by then. "After all, how long can a fish funeral last?"

So that afternoon we went, and stood in a row by the fish cemetery Sara'd laid out. We pretended interest while she scrawled the fish's name in pink crayon on the clean "Deaths" page in her white Bible, then read the Twenty-third Psalm in a slow, dramatically lowered voice.

"Yea, though I walk . . ."

"Swim," Rennie whispered sideways to me.

". . . through the valley . . ."

"Through the muddy little pool," Rennie smirked.

And so on, until finally Elijah and I were snorting to keep from laughing. Sara lifted the veil of the old black hat of Gram's she was wearing, and stared at me reproachfully, so I straightened up as best I could.

When the silly little service was over and the matchbox coffin had been buried with a spoon and the dirt above it covered with about a trillion dandelions, Sara made an announcement.

"The funeral party shall retire to the porch to blow petunia bubbles for the remainder of the afternoon."

Even Elijah rolled his eyes at that. "I'll pass, Sara. I've got . . . things. Things to do."

"Ditto," Rennie snarled, shaking his head as he left.

I shrugged. "I think I'd better get busy in my loft, too."

That was the last time that month that Sara made an open bid for our attention. I think she finally got the message—none of us was going to sit still while she showed off her skills for us.

It was a real relief being able to more or less ignore her. If I'd owed her something for lying at the picnic, after the fish funeral I told myself I could feel that debt was paid.

Rennie, Elijah, and I spent nearly all our free time together by then, prodding and teasing each other, sharing the things I think we'd all three waited a lifetime to really share with someone else.

The two of them often came with me collecting, and the three of us spent hours bent over the two rapidly filling tables in the hayloft, sorting and analyzing the snakeskins, rocks, and insects we found in the fields and woods.

"You guys!" Rennie yelled one day, and held up a tomahawk head he'd pulled like a potato from the newly cut weeds along the edge of Moccasin Creek. Wade was still brush-hogging along the creekbank, and on his next pass through we flagged him down. He left the tractor running and walked to meet us, wiping his forehead with his red bandanna.

"Well, looky there," he said, taking the smooth stone tool Rennie held out to him and whistling appreciatively. "See the way this field has a little rise in the middle? Your grandpa has long thought this was an old prehistoric Indian encampment. There's been lots of nice arrowheads found hereabouts, though nothing nice as this. I reckon this was worked by the Cahokians, right about a thousand years ago."

Wade gently put the tomahawk in my hands, and I took it and moved my fingers hungrily over its cool, perfect shape. It would have been the star piece in the artifact part of my science collection, but when Wade had gone back to the tractor, I held the tomahawk out to Rennie. "Finders keepers," I told him, reluctantly.

He shook his head and shoved his hands into his pockets. "I don't keep things," he said.

I felt a tiny thrill of excitement, but Elijah stepped forward and took the tomahawk from my hands.

"Start with this," he said quietly. "Keep this."

He pulled Rennie's elbow so that his left hand came from his pocket, and quietly put the tomahawk in that hand. Rennie stood perfectly still for a long time and stared down at his hand as though it belonged to someone else, and I began to remember his room, how empty it had seemed that morning.

"Why don't you keep things, Rennie?" I heard myself whisper. Maybe I knew in the instant I asked it how he would answer.

"It's too . . . dangerous," Rennie said, and swallowed hard. Without raising his eyes, he turned and ran, leaving Elijah and me behind.

But he took the tomahawk with him.

Elijah did by far the most field work, but Rennie and I both helped out too that month—bucking bales, for instance. Also suckering the sweet corn, tearing off the fronds that would draw moisture from the developing ears. That was sticky, itchy work, and there was something about it that made the back of my neck feel tingly the whole time, as though danger was lurking, hidden just inches away. After all, the corn towered over our heads, and was so closely spaced that a few feet into it you were sealed from the outside world in a dense green maze. And the drone of the locusts reverberated within those swaying green walls, and seemed to almost enter your head and get trapped there, turning your thoughts into buzzing insects deep inside your brain.

"Has anyone ever actually gotten lost in a cornfield?" I asked Elijah.

He smiled, but shrugged. "Maybe for a little while," he said.

"Only for a while? I'd think you could get totally disoriented and end up too lost to be found," I told him, shivering in the heat as I moved my eyes over the vast sea of waving cornstalks.

Each of the days we worked on the corn I found myself going a little farther into the field, a little farther from the edge of the vegetable garden which itself edged on the back yard.

And then one day, I lost my bearings and couldn't remember which way I'd come, and which way led back home. The corn stalks waved sharp arms at me, poking me with razor fingers. The locusts became louder and my head throbbed. I ran, but the roots of the corn stuck up footlike from the dust and tripped me, so I fell, scraping both knees and jamming my left wrist. I sat there in the dust, and the corn seemed to be bending toward me, laughing.

"Rennie!" I screamed in total panic. "El-i-jah!"

And then I heard a fierce swishing and the crack of corn stalks breaking, and seconds later I saw the flash of Rennie's yellow t-shirt approaching from my left. Elijah appeared in the distance on my right, coming as quickly as Rennie but more carefully dodging the plants.

"Hey, it's okay! It's okay!" Rennie said, as they pulled me to my feet. "Why'd you come so far out?"

I took a deep, shaky breath, but Elijah answered for me.

"She couldn't resist seeing if she could get lost. She can't resist an experiment."

That was the exact truth, though till I heard him say it I hadn't known it.

"What I don't get, though, Tory," Elijah continued, "is why you panicked just now. Seems like you trust nature too much to let a little corn scare you like that."

I took off my glasses and began smearing sweaty dust all over them as I wiped them on my t-shirt. "But the corn became people," I blurted, my words like a sob.

My parents, Sara, my teachers—anybody I could think of would have laughed and told me not to be so silly, that neither corn people nor flesh and blood people would ever hurt me.

But neither of the boys said a word. Elijah just solemnly took my glasses from me and carefully began wiping them off, and Rennie took my elbow and began leading the way out of the field.

The wheat harvest was late that year and in full swing by mid-July. Grandpa and Wade hitched the biggest tractor to the gravity flow wagon, pulled it near the combine each day, and let the combine fill it with newly cut wheat. Then they'd pull the wagon to one of the tall storage bins that stuck up from the fields like hotel-sized silver bullets. As Grandpa watched from the tractor, Wade turned the release wheel on the wagon to let the grain flow through the funnel, out the hatch, and into a long snakelike machine beside the storage bins called a grain auger. Using a mechanical spiral, the grain auger moved the wheat upward through its long cylindrical body, then out its serpent mouth and into the opening high up on the bin.

The wagon was moved each day to wherever the combine was, so I never knew where that huge tyrannosaurus rex would be, and I always got a quick shiver when I looked across a field and happened to see it, grazing in the sunlit distance. Every time I looked at it I remembered the fight that wagon had caused between Elijah and Rennie, and I was glad it was acres away from us now. Still, I didn't think Rennie would try to rimwalk the wagon again.

A lot had changed. We were all three past having to prove things to each other now.

Chapter 21

Elijah, Rennie, and I saw the boy in the window five times during July, always when we were all three together, every time but once at twilight. We went to the cemetery three or four times and looked all over for Americus' grave. It just plain wasn't there, wasn't anywhere in the area of his parents' graves or the old graves of his sisters and brothers.

We decided to brave the wasps' nests to look through the attic to try and find something about him in the old diaries and photo albums Gram kept up there. There was no mention of him in anything we read, but opening an old trunk, I found something I first took to be just a worn scrap of material.

"Oh, wow," I breathed, gently unfolding the red and gray checked fabric and realizing it was a small quilt, a child's quilt. Elijah came to kneel beside me, and Rennie leaned over our shoulders.

"Look at this," Rennie said, reaching out to trace the embroidered letter "A" with his finger. It was centered in one of the red checks, embroidered in black.

We were sure it had been his, tucked away lovingly by Marcella. My hands, after hers, had been the first to touch it.

The one time that month we saw the boy during bright daylight we were looking for arrowheads near where Rennie had found the tomahawk. We were standing in nearly the identical place I'd crossed Moccasin Creek when I first saw the boy, on Memorial Day.

"Look!" Rennie demanded.

Something in his voice made Elijah and me automatically look not to Rennie but toward the old house, toward the round window. And sure enough—there was the boy, clearer at this distance than we'd seen him before. He had both hands and his forehead on the glass and was leaning toward us like small children do when they're forbidden to play outside but want to in the worst way.

Sara's words came into my head—"Poor boy, he's lonely."

Rennie immediately jumped the creek and ran toward the house through the stubble of newly cut hay. Elijah and I followed, but the boy had disappeared from the window by the time we reached the edge of the overgrown yard. Still, none of us would be the first to chicken out, and we went very carefully, room by room, through the house that day for the first time since Memorial Day.

When we'd checked every corner of the upstairs, Elijah sat down on the floor of the landing at the top of the stairway and leaned back against the tattered wallpaper. Rennie and I waited to see if he'd stand back up, and when it was obvious he didn't intend to for a while we sat down near him, so we formed a little circle there with our knees just inches apart.

For a while we didn't talk. I think we were listening to the silence of the house.

"Are you scared?" Elijah finally asked, looking at me.

"Not of this," I answered.

Rennie looked quickly toward me. "Of what, then?"

I pulled my knees up, wrapped my arms around them, and bounced my chin. "I guess of what you said, Rennie, that day you came up to my lab the first time. You said I hid in my lab. I'm scared of not being pretty or very talented and not being able to chatter about stuff like Sara does."

I was surprised at how easily those words had slipped out of me, after so many years of not even letting them be formed.

Rennie began peeling a long strip of wallpaper slowly from the wall. "Wonderful Sara," he murmured. "Sara without an 'h.' "

He frowned, concentrating on the wallpaper as the rip he was making traveled upward, upward.

"One of my dad's new kids, the one in junior high, is named Sara without an 'h,' " he said. "The other one, the one in high school, is named Jason."

I held my breath, totally taken by surprise, hoping he would go on.

Elijah didn't move, but I could see his eyes shift to Rennie, and his brows move quickly downward in a puzzled expression. We both knew about Aunt Crystal's divorce two years before, but I hadn't known till that second, and I don't think Elijah had either, that Rennie's dad had remarried and had a new family.

The paper rip reached the ceiling, and a little shower of plaster dust fell on us like snow.

"Winter is coming," Rennie said, jerking the paper slightly to give us another shower, obviously joking to change the subject.

"No way!" Elijah took the hint, jumped up, and bent over to brush the dust out of his hair and off his sleeves. "And I'll prove it. Last person out of here has to clean up the watermelon mess when we're done pigging out!"

Rennie and I had been waiting for days for Elijah to decide that the watermelons in Gram's garden were ripe enough to eat. Elijah was already headed down the stairs, and Rennie got to his feet and quickly followed him.

"Hey, wait for me!" I tried to make my voice sound jokey, but I hated being alone upstairs for even a second. I couldn't help taking a last uneasy glance into the room where I'd seen—or thought I'd seen—the moving shape almost two months before.

Rennie caught his heel clumping down the stairs, and from where I was a few steps behind him, I thought I saw the stair give in a funny way, bounce slightly and fall back down, almost like the lid of a box.

But I was at least as anxious as the boys to get back out into the sunshine, so I didn't take the time to check it out, and after that split second I didn't think another thing about it.

Back at the house that afternoon, Rennie and I waited by the fence while Elijah crouched in the garden, solemnly thumping melon after melon.

"Hurry, Elijah, we're about to liquefy and evaporate!" I finally complained, and he smiled indulgently and settled on two of the dark green melons. He took one into the refrigerator in the kitchen, and hefted the other one to his shoulder.

Rennie and I followed him to the pond, where he carefully placed the watermelon on a tree stump, then took his pocketknife and carved us all huge half-moon slices.

"Dig in," he instructed.

"Shouldn't we have brought spoons?" I asked. "Or forks?"

"What a sissy!" Rennie laughed as he dipped his face into the rich red fruit and came up with his mouth loaded and dripping. A spot of red clung, also, to his nose.

"Don't take such big bites," Elijah warned him. "Makes it impossible to spit."

He demonstrated, taking a bite half as big as the one Rennie had taken, then sending a stream of seeds like slow bullets toward the poor curious bullfrogs who were poking their heads above the surface of the pond, staring at us.

I took a rubber band from my pocket, fastened my hair back out of the way with it, grabbed my slice of melon firmly between my hands, bent my knees, and issued a challenge.

"I'll show you who's a sissy. Race you! Ready, set . . . go!"

We all three buried our faces and, gulping, dripping, and slurping, polished off those first slices of watermelon in mere seconds. All three of us finished pretty much simultaneously.

"But I'm the winner, because you guys were one bite up on me when we started," I informed them.

"Fair enough," Rennie said, stretching. He kicked off his shoes, then waded into the water.

Elijah and I stayed behind, trying to make a cover for the unused half of the watermelon from our three picked-clean rinds. I felt sticky, sweaty, full to bursting, and perfectly contented.

"He took Sara without an 'h' and Jason on a trip to Colorado this summer," Rennie suddenly said, his back to us. I looked up to see the water gathered like a smooth metal surface at his knees. "When I was a little kid he always promised that we, he and I, would do that, that we'd see the Rockies. But this summer, he's actually doing it, hiking and camping in the mountains. But not with me. With them."

The shine of the afternoon seemed to dull at Rennie's words, and my throat felt tight as I watched him standing as though trapped in that shallow water.

"Where . . . where did you learn to rimwalk then?"
I finally asked, because neither Elijah nor I knew what
else to say. "Did your father teach you in some . . .
other mountains?"

Rennie waded slowly out of the water, and stepped
into his shoes. He crouched to lace them up, and kept
his eyes on his hands.

"My father took a swing at me a few times—other-
wise, he took me nowhere. He didn't like me much
after I quit being little and cute. I practice at night, at
the schoolyard. I walk the top of the chain-link fence,
mostly. Sometimes I scale the bricks of the school—
it's three stories, good traction. When a patrol car
passes, I drop and hide. I work on myself by myself,
alone."

Rennie finished tying his shoes and stood up, but
wouldn't look at me or Elijah. Instead he made a big
production of looking at his complicated watch,
squinting at it, frowning, setting one of the little tim-
ers. Elijah figured out, a second before I did, that this
was a signal that he was getting ready to run.

"Stop," Elijah said, stepping in front of Rennie.
"Don't take off this time."

Rennie looked shocked and almost afraid, and I
realized Elijah was on to something. Rennie liked to
run away almost as much as he liked to rimwalk.

For several seconds, maybe a full minute, Elijah
and Rennie stared at each other. Rennie finally took a
deep breath, let it out, and shrugged. "Fine," he said.
"I can do that. I can stay."

Chapter 22

The last week in July, Sara made herself a tent playhouse in the apricot orchard, stringing some of Gram's old quilts among the branches. All month she'd been gathering the hard, knobby, softball-sized things that grew on the hedge trees along the gravel road. She'd spent days drawing faces with markers on those sticky green hedgeapples, so now she moved her hedgeapple people into the playhouse with her, along with her Raggedy Ann, whose face looked deeply scarred by the blue-turning-gray stains under her eyes. When it rained, Sara collected the rainwater that dripped from the drainspout beside the porch in some battered pans Gram gave her, then took that rainwater into the playhouse, too.

Several times she invited me to visit her "for tea," but I managed to avoid doing it.

When I finally did visit the playhouse, early in August, it was for a very sad reason. It was because on August second, Mr. Effingham died.

Gram, Grandpa, Wade, Sara, and I went to his funeral. It was in the little white clapboard Congregational Church down the road from McKendree Chapel Cemetery, and the sky out the open windows was the simple washed blue of Mr. Effingham's unforgettable eyes.

I glanced at Sara during the service and saw that she had her hands in her lap and was looking down at them, making her two index fingers talk to each other like tiny dolls, moving her lips soundlessly.

"Sara?" I whispered, and when she looked up at me her eyes were filled with tears.

"If his thumb had even part of a soul they would have said a little sermon for it and buried it, wouldn't they?" she whispered back. "They wouldn't have taken any chances."

"Oh, Sara." I took one of her hands in mine and held it tight. She leaned against my shoulder.

I said an awful thing as we drove the short distance home from the church. I didn't mean it the way it sounded—I was just trying to lighten things for Sara, to make her less pale and quiet.

"Well, at least now you won't have to eat that awful candy Mr. Effingham liked so well."

She didn't answer, but Gram turned to me.

"Oh, Victoria, surely you know Mr. Effingham didn't like that candy himself," she said gently, but with a hint of reproach. "He had no teeth—he couldn't possibly have eaten it. He spent what little

167

extra money he had on that candy in case a child, like Sara, happened by."

I felt flustered, and blundered on. "Then why didn't he get a better kind, a kind Sara liked?"

Gram smiled, and sighed. "Because Sara pretended to like it. You did too the day you went to see him, didn't you? So as not to hurt his feelings?"

"Yes," I whispered, feeling clumsy, feeling awful and rude.

Sara disappeared into her quilt playhouse as soon as we got home, and later that afternoon I went in search of her there.

"You okay?" I asked, ducking my head into the soft fabric slit that was her front door.

"Yes," she answered. She was sitting on an old sofa pillow. There were three or four raggedy pillows in there that Gram must have given her.

"May I come in?"

"Yes. Sit there, on the love seat."

A thick, gnarled branch of the apricot tree swooped down in one corner and made a natural sitting place, almost wide enough for two people. Plenty wide enough for one person and a doll.

I sat, obediently. "Nice place," I told her. I couldn't decide how complimentary to be. Was she serious about this being a house, like she had been when she'd strung blankets across the dining chairs at home several years ago? Or did she realize how juvenile this was, and if I took it seriously and overcomplimented would she be offended? The Sara from last spring would be furious if I hinted that she still really played house, with dolls.

"Thanks," she said. "Tea?"

She was offering rainwater, from an old aluminum pan.

She was serious, then. I felt annoyed, and sad, and guilty, and irritated because I felt guilty.

"Sara, why don't you practice your music? Or your cheerleading routines for this fall? You're . . . you're wasting so much time and energy this summer."

"Oh, but you must try the tea!" Now she was using her formal playing-house voice, from when she'd been . . . eight? Seven? "And you simply MUST see my new china."

She pulled a shoebox over beside her. Inside were a bunch of mussel shells from the creek. She looked them over carefully, her finger on her cheek, and chose two.

"Cream?" she asked, as she poured rainwater into them.

I stood up, hunched since the playhouse wasn't very tall.

"I'm not playing, Sara," I told her, my voice shaking a little. "And you're too old to play babyish games like this, too. What in the world is the matter with you, anyway?"

A big part of me hoped she wouldn't answer, or at least not honestly. But she did.

She looked at me steadily, her eyes tear-filled but more quiet and solemn than I'd ever seen them. "You didn't let me come with you that day we picked up hickory nuts," she said evenly. "You and Elijah and Rennie never want me around."

I caught my breath. "We're . . . older, Sara. That's all. Just . . . just into things you'd think were boring."

She picked up the box of shells, looked down into it, and began shaking it, swirling the shells so they clattered together.

"A house shakes when it gets empty," she said. "Like the old corn crib by the flower garden—it shakes when I walk into it. Mr. Effingham's living room shakes when I walk into it too, and the glass in the bookcase tinkles. I go on tiptoe, and still it shakes a little."

I crouched down beside her, and touched her hand to make her quit moving the box. The shells were making a monotonous rattle that shook my nerves— the sound of something alive that shouldn't be. She put down the box and looked quickly up at me, as though surprised to see me there.

"But his house doesn't shake when Mr. Effingham walks through," she said quickly, leaning forward, confiding in me. "One day Gram said Mr. Effingham has been like a shadow since his wife died. I guess shadows don't need much furniture, and don't make things shake when they go by."

I licked my lips, but couldn't think of a thing to say. The un-Saralike way she was dwelling on shadows and gloom was giving me the creeps.

She lifted up one edge of the quilt beside her, and

looked out over the clover field, toward the old house. "Victoria, does heaven start at the tops of the clouds, or higher up?"

"I don't know, Sara," I whispered. "Higher, I guess. But I don't know."

She dropped the quilt, and began talking her index fingers, like she had in the church. "I'm very, very lonely trapped in this old dirty house because no one likes me," her left finger said, in a tiny pathetic voice. "Oh, my dear, I know how you must feel, like a puny old shadow. Won't you have some tea?" her right finger answered.

"Now, Sara, stop that!" I grabbed both her wrists and held them tightly. "You're being babyish and selfish. You brought your trombones, so practice! Or study for next fall, or start a collection for a science project! Good grief, it's just not fair for you to . . . to act like this! To make me feel like this the one time people really, really like me and want to include me! It's not fair! Back home everybody will worship you again, but right now it's . . . it's my turn, Sara! My turn!"

I threw her hands back to her like I would have thrown something burning away from myself, and stood up and jerked out of the playhouse, tearing it partway down in my anger.

I felt dizzy from the dampness inside the tent, and I bent double in the cooler outside air and pushed my hair from my hot face, trying to calm down. Sara slipped from the tent and stood quietly behind me. I turned to her, expecting she would be glaring at me or crying, expecting she would want an apology for the damage to her house.

But she wasn't even looking at me. Her face was calm, far too calm and too expressionless for Sara's bubbly face to ever, ever be. And her eyes were empty as a sleepwalker's and focused on the old house across the fields.

Against my will, I turned and looked where she was looking.

The boy was in the window, solemnly staring right at us.

"He's very, very lonely, but he can't come here," she said softly. "He wants us to come to his house to play instead."

"Sara, just shut up!" I whirled around toward her, echoing Rennie's shocking words to her the first evening of the summer, ages ago. "Just quit it!"

But she didn't seem to even hear me. She remained as sickeningly calm as before, expressionless as a pretty black-haired doll. Or as a beautiful child who has died far too early.

"His mama won't let him cross the creek," she said in that same eerie, singsong voice.

"Sara!" I grabbed her shoulders and shook her, hard.

"Hey!" she yelled, jerking away from me. Her eyes flashed with anger, a mix of emotions played vividly and colorfully across her face, and I felt weak with relief.

"You tore up my house!" She sprinted around the edges of the tent. "Hey, no fair! You must have knocked the quilts loose when you stood up to leave, so you've got to help fix it!"

"Sure. Yes," I said. I pulled and tugged at the quilts, trying to stop my arms from shaking. Sara evidently didn't remember me yanking down the quilts in anger as I left her house. She didn't seem to remember anything after she'd started talking her fingers.

"Sara?"

"Yeah?"

I wanted to tell her I loved her. I wanted to tell her I was worried about her, and that I loved her, and that she should quit playing such sad and lonely games.

But though it was becoming easier and easier to talk to Rennie and Elijah about my thoughts and feelings, it was suddenly amazingly hard to talk to Sara about them.

We heard the front porch door's loud squeak, and seconds later Gram rang the big iron dinner bell that stood near the goldfish pond.

"Nothing," I said. "Never mind."

Chapter 23

I remember how relieved I was to get inside the brightly lit house that night, and to sit at the dinner table with everyone talking and laughing around me. I tried not to glance at Sara and even scooted my chair a few inches away from hers.

Because to tell the truth, I was suddenly a little afraid of her, and of whatever was going on inside her head. In fact, after that night, I think fear made me avoid Sara in the purposeful way Rennie had avoided her all summer. I no longer caught her eye and smiled during meals, no longer very often tried to make chitchat as we got dressed or undressed in our room, no longer gave her much token attention even when Gram brought me up short about it.

I guess the only way I could deal with Sara right then was to just pretend she wasn't around.

August doesn't feel endless, like June and July do. ''What's today's date?'' Elijah asked out of the blue when he and Rennie and I were up in the hayloft one afternoon.

"The seventh, why?" I replied, wishing he hadn't asked.

"In July you could never remember the date when I asked you. Neither could Ren."

"Well, time's back with us." Rennie's voice was quick and sharp, as usual, but by then I could hear past the obvious. His words held definite sadness as he shoved back from the collecting table and went to stand in the window. He grabbed the wooden sides and leaned far forward into the thick light. "Tick, tick, tick. Days gone, days left till . . . school."

I looked at Rennie framed like an about-to-fly Peter Pan in the bright window, and wished with all my heart I could freeze time like lucky Peter had somehow managed to do.

Then I glanced at Elijah, and he was smiling broadly. I realized, then, that Rennie had just said "till school." Rennie the dropout was planning on going back to school this fall! I returned Elijah's smile and gave him a thumbs-up sign, which Rennie caught as he turned around.

"Okay, okay," he muttered, clearly embarrassed, but smiling. "I guess if you two guys can hang in, I can too. Maybe it's time I proved I'm not as stupid as some people think."

Elijah shook his head in a quick, angry gesture of disgust. "Hey, man, if by 'some people' you mean

175

your dad, and if he really thinks that, then HE'S the stupid one."

This kind of sharp opinion was very unusual coming from soft-spoken Elijah, and Rennie met his eyes and held them.

"Thanks," he finally said, and swallowed. "Really, thanks."

Maybe time seems sweeter when there's not much left of it, because my memories of those next two weeks, the second and third weeks of August, are the best memories of my life.

Each day the sun cast sharp-lined shadows behind Elijah, Rennie, and me as we rambled through the fields and woods—teasing, challenging, drifting, dreaming, not talking much or talking excitedly all at the same time, finishing each others' thoughts. The hay was baled and stored, the wheat harvest was over, the soybeans and corn wouldn't be harvested till September and October, so there wasn't as much work around the farm as there had been. We were free nearly all day to follow our own plans, or to just knock around together, happily planless, footloose.

It became part of our daily routine to swing by the old house to look for the boy, whom we hadn't seen since Sara and I saw him that awful night outside the playhouse. The air was slightly cooler and someway softer than it had been in mid-July, and the sun's glare against the round window had turned from the bright yellow of early summer to a deep, burnished gold.

One day we lay on our backs in the tall weeds outside the old house, all three squinting up at that golden window.

"My science medal looks like that," I murmured. "Round and gold. Fake gold. Painted metal. Flimsy, probably cost about a dime or less to manufacture."

"Why do you do that?" Rennie asked, his voice drowsy.

"Do what?"

"Put yourself down like that," Elijah answered for him. "Why DO you do that? You call yourself gawky, or not pretty. You shrug off praise like you don't believe it. You win an important award and act like it's junk. Why?"

"I don't do that," I said.

"Sure you do," Rennie said, and yawned. "So stop, okay?"

"Okay," I whispered, wondering if they could possibly be right. Was I gawky and untalented in everyone's eyes back home, or mostly just in . . . my own? "I'll try."

One afternoon Wade went to an auction in Mulberry Grove and had the hoods of two old cars in his pickup bed when he came back.

"Anyone up for fishin'?" he asked mysteriously, then spent the afternoon welding those old hoods together, using a diamond-shaped piece of sheet metal like a huge piece of tape where they didn't quite fit together in the middle.

By late afternoon there was a rowboat on the big

willow-lined farm pond. The boat had two peaked ends, each end with the word "FORD" upside down. It was a perfect fishing boat, and the three of us took it out a lot.

Luther always came bounding from the barnyard and caught up with us as we shoved off with an oar, then he stood proudly and stubbornly smack in the middle of the small boat and totally in the way while one of us rowed. I guess Wade must have told him right at the beginning that it would be his boat, he would be the captain.

One clear, hot afternoon, Rennie rowed us to the middle of the deep pond. It was a very calm day, without a hint of breeze, and we didn't drift, just idled there. Elijah threw a fishing line, Rennie leaned forward with his elbows on his knees to read a book he'd brought, and Luther yawned and put his chin on his forepaws for a nap.

I relaxed back into the spoon made by the "nose" of one car hood. I lifted my face to the sun, and let one hand dangle into the muddy water. I raised and lowered my hand, and lazily turned my eyes to watch my fingers move from the clarity of the surface to the murkiness a few inches below. I raised my hand, then dangled it again. Down, deeper, then up. Then far, far down.

"Careful," Rennie murmured. "You could lure snakes, or snapping turtles."

"That's exactly what she's doing. She wants to

know if the turtles or snakes will think her fingers are worms," Elijah said. "She can't resist an experiment, remember?"

They both laughed, and I laughed too and splashed them. "You think you're so smart. Well, I'm sick, sick, sick of you two reading my mind!"

Rennie splashed me back, and Elijah splashed us both until finally we were laughing so much and had the boat rocking so hard that Luther panicked and swam for shore.

That same night, after supper, Elijah and I were husking sweet corn in the yard. I hadn't yet washed my hair, and as I worked it kept falling across my face, smelling like the pond, like catfish and clover and sun.

"A bunch of the neighbors are gathering in the fields across from the cemetery tomorrow to get started setting things up for the Chapel Picnic," Elijah said softly. "Grandpa asked if we wanted to help."

I didn't answer, just kept yanking at the corn husks. It was twilight, the sky was pink and the birds sounded quiet and somehow sad, like they do for a while when the sun goes down.

The Chapel Picnic, Irishtown's annual farewell to summer.

"Excuse me," I finally mumbled, and ran away, out of his sight, around the edge of the machinery shed, then on through the fields and clear past the pond. When I was out of breath I fell to earth, surrounded by tall wild wheat and meadow weeds.

The sky had become light navy and a thin little translucent wedge of moon was rising.

Elijah had been only partway right about me—I loved experiments, but I feared what I couldn't know. Until this summer, my fear had outweighed my curiosity, and I had never tested the deep waters, never tempted the monstrous and wonderful things that lived beneath the surface world that I could clearly see around me.

At the beginning of this summer I would have kept my hands in the boat, but never again.

"Please, I don't want the fall to come! Please!" I pleaded in a whisper with the moon. It didn't answer, of course, so I just sat up and hugged my knees for a long time, looking at the lighted house, tiny in the distance, beautiful as an illustration in a book that you can turn to over and over again, all your life.

Chapter 24

The next morning Elijah, Rennie, Wade, Grandpa, and I drove to the big empty fields between McReynold's hog farm and McKendree Chapel Cemetery. When we got there lots of people were already working, and we helped unload the wood several had brought in their pickup trucks, wood they stored in their barns and used to build stands for the picnic year after year.

We went back for several hours every day that week to help hammer together food stands for ice cream, fried chicken, pies, drinks, and hot dogs. There also had to be a big stage, complete with sound system and lights overhead, for the local country musicians with their fiddles, electric mandolins, and guitars. There had to be a huge rectangle of tables and benches to seat a couple hundred people at a time for the bingo game, with lots of room inside for the prizes donated by Mulberry Grove merchants, and for several people to move about passing out cards and handfuls of corn to mark them with. There had to be smaller stands for the other, less important games—balloon and dart games, goldfish bowls you could throw a dime in and win a fish, games where somebody tried to guess your weight or height. And long strings of lights had to be strung from all of the trees, and through all the stands, since the picnic was always held at night.

We didn't build a stand for what Grandpa described as everyone's favorite game, the cakewalk, and one night at dinner I asked Gram why.

"Well, we need no cakewalk stand because Junior McPherson always lends his double hay wagon, and his wife Jean Ann tacks thirty numbers all around the edges. We display the dozens of beautiful donated cakes on tables set up on the wagon. Then Reverend Fisk will step to the table and lift up a cake, and everyone pays fifty cents for a number, and Hessie Simonsen plays piano, and those who've paid for a number walk around the edges of the wagon till the music stops."

"Then Reverend Fisk's daughter Priscilla draws a number and whoever's standing by it wins the particular cake the Reverend is holding up," Grandpa interrupted, sopping up gravy with a biscuit and not looking at Gram. "And then when all the cakes are finally sold, all the old neighborhood women gossip over who baked the best-looking cake and whose wasn't up to snuff, and some get in such a lather they hardly speak to each other till clear the next year."

"Oh, Franklin, don't be so silly," Gram said

briskly. "Now who would take cakes so seriously? Even though the picnic cakes are the best effort of every cook in this county, and every cake is a master-piece, or intended to be."

I bit the insides of my cheeks to keep from smiling when she said that, because I could tell by the way she straightened her back that she'd been in on her share of cake gossip, too.

"None, of course, can match your grandmother's angel food," Grandpa said softly, slipping me a sly wink.

"Well," Gram said, sitting up even straighter. "There's some that would agree with you, Franklin, and I say that in all modesty."

A couple of times as we helped build stands that week Rennie slipped away, across to the cemetery to search yet again for Americus' grave.

"We could have missed something, a really small marker, or one with the name almost worn off," he whispered to Elijah and me the first time he went. "You guys stay here or everybody will wonder what we're doing."

As it was, I noticed Wade watching Rennie both times, a tiny pucker of a frown between his two red eyebrows.

The afternoon before the Chapel Picnic I climbed up to my lab and nearly stuck my head right through an immense spider web that suddenly stretched clear across the opening at the top of the ladder. At the web's center was a gorgeous yellow and black garden spider the size of the palm of my hand. She was in the process of embroidering a thick zigzag of white, zipperlike, down the center of her web.

I'd been hoping all summer for a spider like this one to watch. I carefully slithered on my stomach under the web, then lay on my side on the floor, propped on an elbow, admiring her work.

After a while, my eyes drowsily refocused. I looked out the window through the web, toward the green, waving soybean fields, and beyond them, the wheat fields. Where the combine had passed through the wheat during the harvest in July there was greenish stubble. I sleepily remembered how the combine had looked going through the wheat, leaving stubble on one side and on the other a straight edge of gold so thick it looked like the world itself had been sliced away two feet below it.

There was old tyrannosaurus rex, too. The gravity flow wagon was still in the fields, filled with the last load of wheat, waiting for someone to get around to unloading it into the storage bin that stood nearby.

My eyelids felt heavy, and closed. My elbow collapsed, and my arm pillowed my head.

All summer the boy in the window had stood in the silence and shadows just at the edge of our sunshiny world. Tonight the people of Irishtown would bring music and laughter and strings of light to the edge of the cemetery. In a way we would be the outsiders as the boy had been all summer. At the Chapel Picnic, where light met darkness, would we finally learn the truth about the waving boy?

When I was so close to sleep that I couldn't tell if I was dreaming, that question drifted through my mind like a message tumbling through the dark ocean in a bottle.

Chapter 25

Grandpa and Wade worked outside later than they meant to that afternoon, and it was nearly nine o'clock and totally dark by the time we finally left for the Chapel Picnic. As Grandpa pulled the station wagon from the long driveway onto the gravel road, we could see a halo of light against the black sky over the picnic area on the cemetery hill, two miles away. Boiling light, full of smoke and country music.

We drove past the old house, and it seemed to glow slightly, as though still holding the sunshine from the hot day. The brambles and bushes were a jagged dark fringe along its bottom.

On down the road we turned, and began the drive up the steep slope of McKendree Hill. Our headlights were reflected back by some of the shiny tombstones as we approached the cemetery.

''Does Uncle Harley's monument need weeding?'' Gram asked.

"Those aren't weeds," Rennie said. "Just shadows."

The wind came up, and a sprinkle of yellow elm leaves fell in front of our lights, then crunched beneath our tires. Grandpa took a sharp right at the crest of Chapel Hill Ridge, away from the dark cemetery and toward the bright lights of the makeshift parking lot and the picnic beyond it. Only the narrow dirt road separated one thing from the other.

Gram had told us that everyone from the whole county came out on picnic night, and there was a sea of cars—hundreds of them. Past the cars we could see long lines of people at the fried chicken stand, crowding the benches under the swaying strings of lights of the bingo game, and walking in groups, laughing and talking in an animated, exaggerated way in order to be heard above the amplified music coming from the bandstand.

Everything on the picnic side of the tiny road was so—alive.

Rennie, Elijah, and I were sharing the backseat, and Rennie leaned across Elijah to whisper to both of us.

"I've got something to show you guys. In the cemetery."

As though overhearing, though I don't think she could have, Sara turned and bounced onto her knees to lean toward us over the front seat.

"Grandpa says you have to stay with me tonight. You can't go anywhere unless you have me along."

Her whiny tone of voice made Rennie glare out the window to show his disgust with her.

"Didn't you say that, Grandpa?" Sara asked, quietly and defensively.

"No need for any of you to wander around alone in this crowd," Grandpa replied. "Best to stick together on picnic night."

But we did shake free of Sara.

We slipped quietly off when she was standing with Gram up on the cakewalk wagon, oohing and aahing over a cake decorated like the skirt of a doll, with a real doll stuck inside it.

I remember thinking about Grandpa's instructions, but telling myself that Sara wasn't alone, she was with Gram. And the three of us weren't alone either. We were never alone any longer.

I had the strangest sensation of going from one dimension to another that night as Elijah and Rennie and I ran across the skinny dirt road separating the parking lot from the cemetery. It only takes the movement of an eyelid for light to fall to darkness. It only takes a split second for noise to drop to total silence. I don't think I'd realized how thin the border was between those opposite things until we crossed into quiet darkness that night, and it made me feel excited someway. It made me notice the snap of every twig beneath our feet, the glimmer of every firefly.

"Hurry!" Rennie called back to us as we skirted the dark tombstones, running breathlessly and recklessly.

The needles of the old ragged cedar trees that grew thick in the cemetery were almost lost, blotted into the sky like ink. It was a very dark night, and the wind seemed to make it darker.

Then the thin white limestone markers of the older graves appeared ahead, reflecting the dim light of the distant picnic far more clearly than the newer, more ornate monuments had. Rennie reached that part of the cemetery and stopped so abruptly Elijah nearly ran into his back.

"Here," Rennie whispered. "Right here, under my feet. There's no stone or marker, but you can see a cleared place, a little circle without much grass and slightly sunken."

We all three dropped to our knees, felt the ground, and learned by touch what our eyes hadn't noticed in daylight. Rennie was right—there was an area less than four feet long that was nearly grassless and a fraction of an inch lower than the ground around it. It was more of an oval than a circle.

"What . . . what's that?" Elijah said suddenly, and jumped to his feet, looking back toward the picnic.

My heart slammed. Rennie and I followed Elijah's eyes and scrambled up too.

Against the bright cartoon of the distant picnic loomed a dark shape, small but becoming larger, heading, slowly, right toward us.

A short, exuberant shadow bounced along beside it.

"Relax," I said, letting out my breath in a hoarse laugh. "It's Wade. See? That's Luther with him."

The three of us sank down and sat around the oval

189

again, all a little spooked, all breathless with the danger of the night, all bound close by the darkness and laughing at ourselves.

Luther, recognizing our scent, came bounding forward. But Wade just came along slowly and silently, and when he finally reached us he only gave the slightest of nods as a greeting, then stood over us, hands deep in his pockets, staring down at the oval of ground.

My eyes had finally adjusted to the darkness enough so I could see the features of his face fairly clearly, though his eyes were holes of darkness. He seemed so solemn, which was unlike him. Even Luther was subdued, and just lay on the ground by Wade's feet, his paws up covering his nose.

"I see you found what you been looking for," Wade finally managed to say.

"How did you know what . . ." Rennie began.

"Americus, right?" Wade interrupted, and eased himself down beside us. He took in a breath and let it out as a low whistle between his teeth, pulled up one boot to rest his elbow on his knee, and ran a hand through his hair. "I figured after you all said you saw the boy in the window that you'd get your Gram to talking, and she'd tell of Americus. And I figured when Rennie was out here last week he was trying hard to find him, and so he did. Right here is where me and your granddad buried little Americus Simon McNeill."

"But you couldn't have!" I protested. "Gram said

Americus died way, way before she was born! It must have been nearly a hundred and thirty years ago!"

"I don't get this, Wade," Elijah said quietly, picking up on something in Wade's tone of voice. "You said you thought the boy in the window was just a mirage, but I've got a feeling that wasn't the whole truth."

A gust of wind came up, and cedar needles fell on us like sharp, stinging rain.

"No, not the strict truth," Wade agreed softly. "And if there is such a thing as strict truth, maybe I'd just best try to say it now. And maybe I'd best start at the beginning."

Chapter 26

"When I was a young'un, the age of you all now and younger, I used to come up from my pa's farm in the riverbottom to help out in the summers at your Gram and Grandpa's. Your parents were about my age—Crystal, Lydia, and Randall. We had some real good times, working and then playing or more often playing while we worked. The four of us used to love to pass the time by telling ghosty stories, and when your Gram accidentally told us one day about Americus, that got to real quick-like be our favorite. But like you all this summer, we couldn't figure out where he was buried."

"Accidentally? Told you accidentally?" Elijah asked.

Wade reached over and scratched Luther's ears.

"What I mean to say is, when she started that story I could see she was telling it in spite of herself. You understand what I'm saying? She'd been sitting at the kitchen window staring at that old house when we

192

came in to get cleaned up from chores one morning, and she just started talking, like she didn't want to but couldn't not. Like she was talking to herself and not us a'tall.''

"Yes," I whispered, remembering the way she'd told the story to me.

"And after she told about Americus that day, she told your parents and me something else." Wade stopped for a few seconds, and when he started again his voice was husky. "She told that she thought she'd . . . seen him. Seen a face in the window one summer, when she and her sister and two brothers were young. Only that one summer, early in this century, when they were all about the age of you all now, when they were all gathered here together, for the last summer before they scattered. Before her older sister married and left, and her brothers, Frank and Simon, went off to fight in World War I. She told us she was thirteen that summer, the summer they all kept seeing the boy in the window."

"Whoa," Rennie said, sounding like he'd taken a punch to the stomach. "Whoa."

"Really," Elijah whispered.

The wind tossed the cedar trees again, and this time we heard a distant mumble of thunder. The dark sky sputtered brief light along the horizon, and Luther got to his feet and began growling in the back of his throat.

"Easy, old boy," Wade said, then—"I got to stand up. These old legs won't take the damp of the ground." He got up, a little stiffly, and turned his back to us, stared toward the picnic, his hands in his back pockets. Luther dropped to his stomach, wriggled over nearer to him, and put his chin on Wade's boot.

"The summer your Gram told us the story of Americus, we started seeing him, too. We—Lydia, Randy, Crystal, and me—we started seeing a boy in the old round window, waving with his left hand." Wade turned and looked down at us, the expression on his face lost in the shadows. "We saw him that one summer and that summer only, I reckon just like you all are seeing him this summer, but will never any of you see him again."

Chills were passing in waves up my back. "So . . . so you don't believe he's a mirage at all. You believe he's a . . . ghost."

I think that was the first time any of us had dared say that word as a definite possibility.

Wade crouched quickly beside me. "Well now, Victoria, maybe a mirage is all it is. Something growing around that old overgrown place that tricks the eye. Or maybe there's something about a sad memory that can come visible once in a while. Once in a generation, to certain people of that generation. I've thought of lots of maybes to explain it over the years—tricks of the eyes, tricks of the mind, tricks of the heart. But there's one other thing . . ."

He turned his head slowly and stared at the little sunken oval of dirt we were gathered around. All of us looked at it then, at the little unmarked grave.

"Several years ago, your granddad and I went over to seal that old house up for good. We'd been getting afraid that some neighborhood kid would get in and get hurt, so we nailed shut all the windows, put plywood over holes in the floor, that kind of thing. And while we were going upstairs, your granddad caught his boot heel on the edge of one of the steps, and I looked and saw that the wood of that step was warped with dampness, and then I noticed a strange thing. The step was hinged at the top, hinges so covered with dirt you wouldn't have noticed them. That one step was a little sealed box, and we used the crowbar to open it up and found . . . bones. The skeleton of a small child, dressed in old-timey clothes."

We all drew in our breath, and Luther jerked up his head at the sound.

"She couldn't leave him," I whispered. "Marcella couldn't leave her baby behind when she moved from the cabin to the new house on the hill."

"We didn't tell your Gram about it," Wade said quietly. "Your granddad thought it would upset her, so we got permission from the cemetery board and just quietly buried those little bones out here in the old part of the cemetery, close as we could get them to the graves of Marcella and Thomas."

No one said a word then, or moved a muscle. We all sat in that circle and I don't know how much time passed, but I remember I felt a loud buzzing in my ears and only gradually did the sounds of the distant picnic break through it. And then those everyday sounds seemed so strange—how could there be bingo games and lighthearted country fiddling, after what we'd just heard?

Wade stood up, started to leave, then turned back toward us.

"One last thing. I've pondered over this, and I've come to suspect something. If there is, well, a boy, a spirit or memory of him come somewhat real or whatever, I believe it's the energy of a group of people at the start of their best years of life that attracts him, pulls him from wherever he's been. A group of young people from his family, excepting me that time. Two boys, two girls, though that may be coincidence. And it seems to be within the power of that same group to keep him . . . keep him shut outside. Keep him away. I know that's what I felt that summer thirty years ago, and I think your parents felt it too. That he wanted so bad to join us, but that together we were keeping him in his place, in the place where he had to stay. I don't pretend to understand all this, but that's my considered suspicion, and that's all I've got to say."

He stood up and began whistling a little tuneless song through his teeth while he still stared at the grave. Then he turned and began walking back through the darkness toward the picnic light, lifting a hand in a gesture of farewell.

I looked from his retreating back down to Americus' grave again. There was nearly constant lightning along the far horizon now, and the little patch of sunken ground almost appeared to be moving, undulating in the flittering shadows of the wind-tossed trees.

Without a word, suddenly craving the light in every pore of my body, I got up and ran after Wade, and the boys followed me.

"You guys are in real trouble, and I mean REAL!"

We ran into Sara practically the second we crossed the road and got back to the picnic. She was standing by the ice cream stand, evidently waiting for us. Her arms were crossed, her feet planted indignantly, and she had what looked like real tears in her eyes.

"Where's Gram?" I asked, my stomach sinking. "We wouldn't have left you, Sara, but you were with her, at the cakewalk game, and we knew you'd want to stay and play for a while."

"I WANTED to be with YOU guys!" Her bottom lip came out. "I ALWAYS want to be with you, and this time Grandpa said you had to let me, and now you guys are really gonna get it!"

Out the corner of my eye I saw Rennie move toward Sara. I could tell he was angry from the way he seemed coiled up, his fists knotted, his chin pulled in. For an awful instant I was afraid he was going to grab her and shake her, but at the last second he used that energy to jump up onto the thin board that formed one edge of the makeshift ice cream stand. He moved quickly along that rim the length of the stand, looking down at Sara the whole time with rage flashing like sparks from his light eyes.

"Grandpa said you had to! Grandpa said you had to! Why don't you just grow up and quit being such a spoiled brat, Sara?"

He slammed his fist into a clump of helium balloons tied to the corner of the ice cream stand.

"You'll never be one of us, Sara!" He jumped from the stand and landed inches from Sara. "You and your kind can never be Rimwalkers because you haven't got the smarts and you haven't got the guts!"

Rennie ran away, into the crowd, and Sara stood watching him disappear, her face pale, her eyes miserable, helpless, pathetic.

The whole scene had taken perhaps thirty seconds, but it left me feeling sick. I knew Rennie's head had been spinning from Wade's story. His nerves had been on edge, just as mine were, and Sara had just been in the wrong place at the wrong time. Still, Rennie had gone too far. He'd been too mean.

"Sara, I . . ." But what could I say? Apologize for Rennie, say he didn't mean those things when he obviously did?

"Come on, Sara, let's go find Gram," Elijah said. He gently took her hand and she followed him meekly, her head down.

Chapter 27

I can't remember anything about the Chapel Picnic after that. Anything else that happened that night is completely eclipsed in my mind by the horror of the next day, which turned out to be our last day at the farm.

Elijah and Rennie and I did the chores that Sunday morning as usual, though we'd gotten home after midnight from the Chapel Picnic and we all did our work in sort of a sleepy daze.

Then we all went with Gram and Grandpa to Sunday services at the little Congregational Church, also as usual.

We ate dinner, cleaned up, and then everyone scattered as they always did on Sunday afternoon. Everything to that point, early afternoon, was perfectly normal, except for our tiredness and the sharper than normal tension between Rennie and Sara.

Wade announced that he was going to auger the last load of wheat from where it had been sitting in the field in the gravity flow wagon up to the nearby storage bin. Rennie and Elijah asked if I wanted to go fishing, and I said yes but that I wanted to do a little stuff up in my lab first. They said they'd go dig the worms while I did that. Gram fell asleep in her rocker, Grandpa in the hammock in the yard. Sara, the last time I noticed, was playing in her quilt house under the apricot trees.

I climbed into the hayloft, slid on my back carefully beneath the spider, and went to the table to clean and polish some arrow points. One of the barnswallow families had just brought their babies to the edge of their mud-and-hay nest, probably in hopes of teaching them to fly that day. I went over to that dark eave for a closer look—the two babies stared down at me with their bright bead eyes, looking like smug little businessmen, unafraid, chest feathers puffed importantly.

But the parents weren't that calm. I was a terrible threat, and they began flying wildly, trying to scare me away.

One of them looped all through the loft, and suddenly whipped right through the spider's web. The mother bird rocketed back to the nest in surprise, sticky filament trailing from her wings. I ran and knelt by the ruined web in time to see the spider scrambling for cover under a hay bale.

I felt a sick tension spreading through my head as I sat cross-legged by the big window, hoping the spider would come out and begin weaving again. What she'd just experienced would be exactly like having a runaway jetliner crash through your house, destroying it and all your belongings. The birds had been right—I was a terrible threat, whether I'd meant to be or not.

I sighed, rubbed my forehead, and then the strong, golden light from the window drew my eyes outside.

Wade had the tractor out by the gravity flow wagon and was hooking it up to power the grain auger. The grain auger had its serpent mouth inside the opening in the bin, and its bottom end close to the gravity flow wagon, ready to move the grain upwards when Wade turned on the tractor and opened the door beneath the wagon's funnel. The tractor, auger, and wagon made a sort of triangle, with Wade moving from point to point, making connections. More than ever the machines looked to me like a small group of prehistoric beasts grazing in the stubble of the wheat.

I leaned forward to look around the edge of the window, knowing Rennie and Elijah would be digging worms near the compost pile beyond the vegetable garden. Sure enough, Elijah was digging, and Rennie stooped to grab the worms as they tried to wriggle off.

I squinted to refocus my eyes, to look farther away. The trees were waving gently around the old house. The attic window was empty.

And then, suddenly, it wasn't.

Suddenly the boy was there. And at that instant, the

201

golden light seemed to thicken, and I wondered if I was awake or asleep. I felt hypnotized by the droning of the locusts, the warmth of the oak boards beneath my legs. My heart was slamming, but I felt unable to move, or think.

Sara appeared in my field of vision, walking out of the apricot orchard, walking slowly, steadily, dragging her rag doll by the hair behind her. But she wasn't walking toward the old house. She was headed diagonally through the clover, toward the stubbly wheat fields, toward where Wade worked.

Why?

I looked again toward Rennie and Elijah. They could have seen Sara in the distance, but they didn't happen to turn that way. Wade was on the tractor now, starting it. Sara, seeming so small at this distance, kept walking steadily toward Wade and the machines.

I stumbled to my feet, and realized my knees were weak.

Sara walked so steadily, so evenly, like a wind-up toy.

And now both the tractor and the auger were running, and Wade disappeared, behind the wagon, probably to adjust the small hopper that would catch the grain as it fell from the wagon so the grain auger could scoop it up.

Sara kept walking right toward him. I think that was the first time I screamed, though the sound was completely lost, even to my own ears, in the racket being made by the tractor and auger.

Sara reached the machines, dropped her doll, and began climbing the ladder attached taillike to the wagon's back. I could see her clearly, but Wade couldn't have. I knew he couldn't see her or hear her above the bellowing machines.

The four rungs on the ladder were far apart, and Sara had trouble. Twice she fell back, but she kept trying. Finally, she made it to the rim at the wagon's top, and pulled herself up to sit perched there.

My legs were shaking so I couldn't stand very well. I propped myself against the edge of the window and screamed and screamed, soundlessly. Blood hammered in my ears, also soundlessly.

And then Sara was standing, teetering on the edge of the wagon. She was turned outward, toward the boys. She was looking toward Rennie and Elijah, yelling at them, trying to get their attention. Her mouth opened and closed like the mouths of the baby birds, but no sound came out above the sound of the machines.

Rennie's words from last night exploded in my head. *You'll never be one of us, Sara. You'll never be a Rimwalker.*

I grabbed a breath and bolted, then—slid down the hayloft ladder, fell roughly to the ground, stumbled up, and looked frantically back across the fields.

Sara was gone from the edge of the wagon.

My legs became pistonlike as Rennie's. I ran to Grandpa, sleeping under the elm trees, woke him, yelled, and pointed.

And then I plunged through the apricot trees and

made for the wheat field. Rennie and Elijah either saw me or saw Sara as she fell. Anyway, they were running too, and got to the wagon just as I drew close.

I lifted my eyes and saw that the auger was still moving far above our heads, carrying gold to the opening in the bin. Wade didn't know, then, what was happening. Rennie was climbing the ladder on the wagon, moving nearly too fast for my eyes to follow. Elijah was running toward the tractor, jumping onto it, turning it off so the auger lost power and stopped. Silence, and my blood turned to ice. Silence, and the only sound was the sound of the grain falling like sleet into the trough below the funnel.

"Cry, Sara! Cry!" I screamed from beside the monstrous wagon, into that awful silence.

"What?" Wade said, coming from around the bin. "What the dickens is going on?"

"She's not down there!" Rennie yelled from the top of the wagon. "She's totally covered! She's been sucked under the wheat!"

Wade's tanned face turned instantly white, and he and Elijah ran to the opening under the funnel. Rennie jumped down to join them and I forced my legs to move and ran to that side too. Elijah grabbed the wheel above the funnel, and turned fast and hard, opened the door as wide as it would open. The wheat, which had trickled out, came out in a hard, fast avalanche, and Sara came out with it.

She tumbled out with that grain like a limp rag doll. Elijah and Wade yanked her away from the growing mound of wheat, and I fell beside her, began clawing at her mouth and nose, trying to get that awful grain out of her, trying to make her . . .

"She's not breathing," Wade said, quickly and quietly. "We'll give her CPR. You know how, right, Eli?"

"Right," he said, and bent to force open her mouth, to clear her throat with his fingers.

And it was then, then . . .

I raised my eyes, tears blinding me, and looked at the old house. The boy was leaning toward us, both hands on the glass of the round window.

And for the first time all summer, he was smiling.

Chapter 28

"Sara, please!" I sobbed, as Elijah breathed into her, as Wade pumped her chest. "Please, please, please—oh, Sara, don't leave me! Don't die!"

Time hung suspended like the thick, suffocating wheat dust swirling slowly in that golden air.

"She's . . . she's breathing!" Wade suddenly yelled. "She's breathing!"

We all scrambled back a little to give her some air. And Sara coughed, and choked, and coughed. And then . . .

Then she opened her eyes and waved to us, with her left hand, only opening and closing her fingers like a very young child would do, a child too young to know you're supposed to move your whole hand and arm.

And then she closed her eyes again. I ran to her, grabbed her up, and rocked her in my arms, but her eyes wouldn't open.

* * *

Sara was still unconscious when the paramedics arrived in an ambulance and took her to the hospital in Mulberry Grove. From there she was taken by helicopter, with Gram at her side, to St. Luke's Hospital in St. Louis.

When we got back to the farm from Mulberry Grove, Grandpa called my parents.

I huddled with my hands tight over my ears in a corner of the bathroom while Grandpa dialed the phone. I kept chanting some meaningless words. I couldn't stand not to be near while he was talking to Mom and Daddy, but neither could I face hearing his responses to what they said.

It seemed I huddled there for hours, then Grandpa slowly opened the bathroom door a crack. "Sweetheart, your mother's still on the phone and wants to talk to you."

Grandpa helped me walk to the phone, and kept his arm tight around my shoulders as I watched my hand reach to take the receiver.

The overseas line was crackly, and Mom sounded far, far away.

"Oh, honey, are you all right?"

I stood there swallowing, over and over again.

"Victoria, now listen, we all love Sara very, very much and we'll all pull her through this thing, together. And we love you, and . . . and, oh, I wish we were there for you."

Her voice broke, and Daddy took the phone.

"How's my girl?" he asked.

"Oh, Daddy, she won't open her eyes!" I blurted before my throat clamped shut in real, throbbing pain.

"I meant, how are you?" Daddy said gently, hoarsely. "Listen, we'll be on the next plane, and we'll see you by tomorrow. Until then, will you imagine our arms around you? Will you do that for me?"

I couldn't answer, and I felt numb as I handed the phone back to Grandpa.

I walked zombielike out of the house, through the yard, and up the ladder to the hayloft. I took the old broom that had leaned all summer in one dark corner of the loft, and stood there holding it in both hands for a while, watching it wobble as my arms shook and my fingers got white and numb. I was clenching my teeth so hard they crackled. A low growl began in the back of my throat and changed quickly to a howl, and I began whirling around, swinging the broom.

I crushed all my collections that afternoon, slammed and smashed every specimen, every exhibit, even kicked apart the microscope I'd treasured so much, grinding the lens under the broomstick. When everything on the tables was in splinters, I spun around blindly in circles, groaning, slamming the broomstick against the rafters, against the hay bales in the dim corners of the room, only instinctively avoiding the barnswallow nests.

At one point I dimly heard feet hurrying up the ladder.

"LEAVE ME ALONE!" I screamed toward the sound. "I HATE! I just, just hate, hate, HATE . . ."

"What, Tory?" Rennie asked very quietly, rushing to stand right in front of me, grabbing my arms above the elbows. "What is it you hate so much? Just say it. Go ahead and say it!"

". . . myself," I whispered, looking miserably into his eyes.

Rennie released me and collapsed, crouched down, and put his head in his hands. "I thought you were going to say me. That you hated me."

"Rennie!" I was shocked to my senses and knelt beside him to put my hand on his shoulder. I could sense that Elijah was standing quietly somewhere nearby.

Rennie took his hands away from his wet face and slammed clenched fists against his knees. "Why shouldn't you hate me? Everybody hates me, sooner or later. I wreck things. My dad told me that the last time I saw him. I thought if I got strong enough I could prove him wrong, but I see now he was right all along. I . . . I wrecked Sara."

"No! Rennie, it was me! I'm her sister! I should have been the bridge, connected her to you guys. But I think I was . . . afraid. Afraid she'd dazzle you like she dazzles everybody. So I . . . I squeezed her out."

"Stop it, you guys." Rennie and I both jerked our heads toward Elijah's voice. He walked slowly toward us where we crouched in the shadows. The light caught at his jeans, then quickly released them as he passed the window.

"Rennie, you didn't wreck Sara. And Tory, neither

209

did you. None of us wanted to be mean to her, but she reminded all three of us too much of the kids who rule the school at home. We all three had to get away from that this summer. We had to be . . . free. Free to figure out who we were and wanted to be, without kids like Sara always assuming that we wanted to be just like them.''

Elijah's words made me feel slightly calmer. But only for a second, because then I knew it was time to face the awfullest part of what had happened in the wheat field.

''You . . . you guys saw her, didn't you?'' I forced myself to ask. ''You saw her wave when she opened her eyes?''

Elijah took a breath and let it out. ''I saw, yes.''

''And wasn't it exactly the way . . . the way HE always waved?'' I whispered, my voice shaking. ''Wade said if we stuck together we could keep the boy in his place. But we didn't stick together, not all four of us. We three shut Sara out. She kept saying the boy was lonely. What if he lured her to the wagon, called her, made her fall so he'd have a . . . a friend?''

''Wade also said that the boy could just be a memory,'' Rennie said in a rush, obviously wanting to believe that explanation as badly as I did right then. ''Maybe that's all he is, a strong memory trapped somehow in the house. How'd Wade put it?—revived by the energy of a group of people . . . ''

'' . . . At the start of the best years of their lives,'' I finished for him in an aching whisper.

Would Sara even *have* those best years?

Anguish and disbelief rolled through me again in a huge tidal wave, and I put my arms on my knees and tucked in my head. The boys just silently let me cry, until finally I whispered to them that I needed to be alone for a while, and they left.

My tears gradually gave out as exhaustion set in, and I lay back in the dust and stared toward the rafters of the old barn.

My spider, or one just like her, was dangling from a thin line of filament attached to one of those rafters. I watched her twisting slowly above my head until she gradually changed in my mind to a girl. She was me but wasn't me. She could have been anyone.

The dangling girl turned slowly, slowly, facing first one thing and then another. She couldn't have everything, everyone. Not at once, anyway. But she didn't not care about the parts of her world she wasn't facing. She didn't turn her back on anything. She just faced toward things, and her back just automatically followed.

I fell asleep watching the spider-girl there in the shadows.

I woke just a short while later. It was nearly dark. Two things had come clear in my mind. The first was that I loved Sara more than anyone in the world. The second was that I would never be able to regret what Rennie and Elijah and I had had that summer.

* * *

The last thing I saw as I climbed down the ladder of my hayloft for the last time was the spider. She had found the courage to leave the rafters, and was spinning a new web, in the exact place she'd had her first one.

Chapter 29

Since the beginning of August I'd practiced leaving the farm many times in my mind. I expected to make a ritual of it. I thought the boys and I would revisit places to say good-bye, maybe even go again to the Cavendish Crossing Bridge where we'd walked the rim and sealed our close friendship. We'd see things, touch things, for one last time.

But as it turned out, I didn't say good-bye to anything, not even, really, to Elijah and Rennie. I remember the sun was setting as Grandpa and I drove silently to St. Louis that night, to the hospital. But I didn't record in my mind how that sunset looked, or even notice the way the house looked as we drove away.

I did look toward the old house, for the thousandth time that day. The round window was still empty.

As it turned out, I was never to see the little boy again.

* * *

The next few days are a painful blur in my mind. My parents arrived from Ireland, and we all—Gram, Grandpa, Mom, Daddy, and I—spent most of our time hugging and crying, not talking much, holding our breath it seemed, waiting for any word that Sara was improving or getting worse.

And then, on Saturday, Sara awoke.

We were almost afraid to feel too hopeful, afraid to see her and touch her for fear we'd break her and she'd close her eyes and go into that awful sleep again.

"You must understand," the soft-spoken young neurologist explained to us, "the next weeks and months will be slow-going. She may recover completely, but she may be . . . well, a different, or perhaps only slightly different, person than you knew before. There may, in other words, be irreversible brain damage from oxygen deprivation while her heart was stopped. It's simply too early to tell. We'll need to start gradual therapy here, and when she's up to it we can transfer her to a hospital or rehab center near your home in Milwaukee. For now, we'll just watch and see."

I was afraid to go in to see her that first time after she'd awakened. Though her eyes were open and she was making slight movements, she hadn't spoken to anyone yet. She'd barely responded to our parents' caresses and soft words.

Was she waiting? Would she suddenly, at the sight of me, remember everything about this summer, remember the accident and scream an accusation at me, then slip backwards into the darkness?

I crept to the side of her bed.

"Sara?" I whispered.

At the sound of my voice, she turned her head slowly my way.

"Hi," she breathed, and smiled just slightly.

"Oh, Sara." I slipped to my knees, and grabbed her hand in both of mine, putting my suddenly wet cheek against it. "Oh, Sara, are you okay?"

"Hi," she repeated softly, then closed her eyes. But only to rest. I could tell she wasn't slipping back to that awful, lonely place she'd been.

Mom was in the doorway. She'd seen and heard, and her face was filled with relief and happiness.

"We should have known she'd save her first word for you," she whispered into my hair, managing to laugh for the first time all week as I went to her and we hugged each other. "Ever since you girls were toddlers, any time Sara's had any news, she's wanted you to be the very first to hear it."

Mom went in to be with Sara then, and I wandered aimlessly on down the hospital hallway as guilt and relief battled inside me.

By the nurses' station there was a chart on the wall, a poster really. It had probably been there all along, I'd probably passed it dozens of times that awful week, but only now did it stop me.

It was a drawing of a human body from the waist

215

up, with all the organs drawn as though the person was transparent.

The heart was near the middle, and all the hundreds of veins and capillaries radiated out from it like spokes from the center of a spiderweb, or like tiny bridges the blood traveled along.

Wonderingly I traced part of that fragile network with my finger, thinking of how life itself walks along tiny rims inside us, not knowing anything at all for sure about what will happen next. Just moving constantly ahead, one surge of the heart at a time.

Sara spent the next two months in St. Luke's, and then came home to spend a month in a rehabilitation center in Milwaukee. She didn't start school with her class; instead she spent the rest of that year at home. Physical therapists and speech therapists came to our house to work with her. Mom, Daddy, and I worked with her too, took her constantly through her old school lessons, making a big deal of each little bit of progress she made, trying to hide our own fear when she exploded in angry frustration because things that had once come so easy to her now came so very hard.

Meanwhile, that year that Sara was recovering in the hospital and at home, I started high school. I'd expected to feel insecure and nervous around my classmates, as usual. But instead I found myself looking people in the eye, even trying out for and making the volleyball team. It seemed natural to compete, to risk, now. To break free from my laboratory hiding place, to experience all of the jumble of life as a sort of huge science experiment. I was flabbergasted to be accepted like I was.

And it intensified the guilt I couldn't help feeling about Sara.

Sara's ease with life had ebbed while mine grew.

How much was I to blame? The question couldn't be answered by any scientific method I could discover, no matter how hard I tried. And I tried hard, tried to puzzle it all out.

I try hard still.

Epilogue

For years I guess I thought time would eventually unravel the mystery of what exactly happened that bright and awful August afternoon. But that doesn't seem to be the way it works. Time turns out to bring more questions about life, love, and death, and the answers seem to get fewer and fewer.

As I write, nearly twenty years have passed since that summer. Gram has been dead for five years, Grandpa for nearly eight. I still drive down from Milwaukee to the farm on Memorial Day each year, to decorate the graves, to check on the old houses.

Gram's house has been empty since her death, and most of the apricot trees are broken and jagged now, mangled by wind and lightning. You can still stand beneath them, though, and look across to where overgrown brambles and huge elm trees completely hide the shell of the old house. Sometimes you can see a glint of reflected sun from near the treetops that tells me the glass in the round window must be still intact.

I'm afraid my grandparents' house will soon be as lost and beyond repair as the older house is. Last year when I visited, two of the big pillars on the porch were broken, like long white bones, snapped.

I stop twice at McKendree Chapel Cemetery when I make my yearly visit to Illinois—once on the way to the farm in the morning, and once as I leave at sunset to begin the long drive back to Milwaukee. I stop in the morning to leave the foil-covered coffee cans I've saved all year, with their bouquets of bright flowers I grow in the little botany department greenhouse near my office at the University. I know Gram would want those flowers left early in the day, so the crowd visiting the cemetery for the holiday has more chance to admire them.

When I stop the second time, on my way home, I put a single white daisy from the bank of Moccasin Creek on the little unmarked grave of Americus McNeill.

Sara, too, still lives in Milwaukee. She is married to a sweet, patient man, and has three children. She's not the Sara of our youth, but she is that Sara's slower, quieter shadow. When Sara finally entered seventh grade a year after the accident, anyone who'd never been dazzled by her vibrant, show-offy ''Saraness'' might have assumed this new, deliberate, careful Sara who very occasionally slurred her words was the only one who had ever existed.

She doesn't remember much about the summer of

219

the accident. She doesn't remember seeing the boy in the window. And there are other strange gaps in Sara's memory. For instance, she never could play trombone after the accident, and she started favoring her left hand over her right.

But in a strange way, Sara's life probably turned out to be changed the least of any of the four of ours by that summer. Rennie, Elijah, and I became hard to recognize as those three insecure kids who met the day before Memorial Day—one perched cockily on the roof, the other two dodging a falling screen below him in the yard.

Rennie stayed in high school, and got good grades because he quit cutting classes. When he graduated he became a fireman in San Diego. Aunt Crystal was very proud and sent us pictures often from the newspapers. You could never tell for sure which fireman he was in those shots of heroic men climbing or hacking their way into burning buildings. You couldn't see faces clearly beneath those heavy hats. But if there was one man climbing higher, balancing more precariously than the others, I knew in my heart that was him.

He was killed fighting a fire when he was twenty-six. Just before he fell to his own death, he rescued two toddlers from the seventh floor of a building. Those toddlers are teenagers now, and Aunt Crystal says one of them, the boy, has Rennie's picture blown up to poster size in his room.

Elijah became a farmer, or continued to be a farmer

I should say, taking over part of his father's land when he got his Bachelor of Agricultural Business degree from the University of Missouri. He's married to a kindergarten teacher, and so far has one son. Elijah rode out the years when so many farmers were going under, and gradually has expanded and diversified his farming operation.

"It's been a mix of savvy and risk-taking at every step," he wrote to me in a letter once. We write fairly often. "The savvy took a lifetime of farming. The risk-taking I had to learn in a crash course, and you know how and when I learned it."

Elijah and I sat together at Rennie's funeral. There were hundreds and hundreds of people there, including the Mayor of San Diego, who read the eulogy. Rennie's father didn't come. Or if he did come, he kept his silent distance, too ashamed to sit with the rest of the family.

Something's just occurred to me. Sara has two girls and one boy. Elijah has one son. If the farm keeps standing, will those four someday meet there to spend a bright summer at the start of their real, true lives? And what will happen then?

I've never married. I became a geologist when I gave up the part of science that dealt with living things. Eventually you have to stop finding dead butterflies for your collections and experiments and actually progress to the point where you kill butterflies and other things, and I couldn't take that step, especially not after that summer.

But I love my rocks and fossils, my archaeology and geology, and I love the sun over my head, painting the air so many colors and densities. I love the layeredness of this old world.

I'm happy, but never as happy as I was that brilliant, golden July, or those early weeks of August. I have a hunch that you can only be that happy once in your life, and then only with lots of luck.

Time brings few certainties, but a few strong hunches. For instance, the older I get the more I believe in the power of memory. I believe that Marcella could have made the memory of her dead son real just by her pain and her love. Just as she saw the sun trapped in her unfinished house on the hill, I believe she could have shamed the house into trapping his warmth, the sound of his laughter, the look of his face. And I believe Wade was onto something when he imagined that a group of people full of new, free energy could stand together inside thick, golden light and resurrect that warmth.

But could that memory of Americus have become real enough to call to Sara, to lure her to the accident that nearly killed her? She definitely became younger and younger that summer. Was it the influence of Americus that made her seem so childish? Or did she become self-centered and babyish in an unsuccessful effort to get our attention?

Did she fall following Americus, or showing off?

The fact I can't escape is that either way, our rejec-